PASSION'S SLAVE

Ramón Torres was accustomed to giving orders and having them obeyed. Those who wronged him, as Grant Leigh had, would feel his revenge . . . Georgia was wild and carefree, riding her motorbike down through Spain for her long-planned rendezvous with Grant, her beloved twin brother. But fate, in the form of Ramón, intervened. Even in her torment, something primitive stirred in Georgia, and Ramón knew it — just as he would always know everything about her . . .

REBECCA KING

PASSION'S SLAVE

Complete and Unabridged

LINFORD
Leicester

First published in Great Britain in 1995

First Linford Edition
published 2007

All the characters in this book have no existence
outside the imagination of the author, and have
no relation whatsoever to anyone bearing the
same name or names. They are not even
distantly inspired by any individual known
or unknown to the author, and all the incidents
are pure invention.

British Library CIP Data

King, Rebecca
    Passion's slave.—Large print ed.—
Linford romance library
    1. Spain—Fiction 2. Love stories
    3. Large type books
    I. Title
    823.9′14 [F]

    ISBN 978–1–84617–643–2

Published by
F. A. Thorpe (Publishing)
Anstey, Leicestershire

Set by Words & Graphics Ltd.
Anstey, Leicestershire
Printed and bound in Great Britain by
T. J. International Ltd., Padstow, Cornwall

This book is printed on acid-free paper

For Emma and Charlotte

1

A long, cool shower — that was what she needed. As yet another bead of sweat trickled down her back, Georgia peeled away her bra, dropped it on the chair on top of the rest of her clothes and picked up her toilet-bag.

But as she turned towards the tiny hotel bathroom there was a fierce flurry of gravel as a car scorched to a halt just outside her basement room. Heavens, someone was in a great hurry on an afternoon of searing Spanish heat, when it was almost too much to put one foot in front of the other. Impelled by a sudden curiosity, she padded across to the closed shutters and, conscious of her nakedness, eased them apart just a crack with her fingertips.

Peering up through the slats, as though through the bars of a prison cell, she could just make out the bottom two-thirds of a car — or, rather, of a sleek pale grey shark. A tanned arm was resting on the sill of the open window, and even from this slanted angle Georgia could see the sprinkle of dark hairs on the back of that arm, glinting in the sun. Four long fingers were beating a staccato tattoo on the grey metal. Everything above, though, was invisible — masked by the huge wooden pergola which, smothered in rampant scarlet bougainvillaea, ran the length of this side of the hotel.

The arm was withdrawn, there was a soft click as the driver's door opened, then the luxurious sigh of a leather seat as a male body eased itself from it, and a pair of knee-high boots emerged, glossy in black patent leather. They were topped by a pair of immaculate cream jodhpurs. Sharkskin — no doubt to match their owner's car, Georgia thought with a faint smile.

Above the black leather belt encircling the waist she could see just a couple of inches of black shirt. One hand was flicking a set of car keys against a thigh, and her eyes travelled slowly across those hard, lean thighs, up to the flat stomach then down the long length of leg, clasped in a close embrace by those sharkskin breeches. Uncompromisingly masculine: the face was invisible, but no one could possibly mistake the owner of such a pair of legs and hips for anything other than a male of the species.

Hmm. Quite a lower half . . . Wonder what the top half is like? she thought idly. With her little finger she opened the shutter a fraction more, but the rest of the stranger stayed stubbornly invisible as he walked across to where her motorbike was parked. The black patent boots stood motionless, then walked slowly all round it, and her stomach muscles tightened with alarm. But then surely a man who drove a car like that would hardly need to steal a motorbike, even if it was a highly collectable vintage Rudge-Whitworth?

Next moment, another pair of legs

appeared — those of the taciturn middle-aged woman who'd signed her in at Reception a few minutes earlier, to judge from the dark flowered skirt. There were voices, first the woman's, then the man's — curt, harsh-edged, a voice accustomed to giving orders and having them instantly obeyed.

A moment later he swung on his heel and strode off out of Georgia's line of vision, the woman pattering after him. Oh, well, she never would be able to put a face to that body now — unless he was a fellow guest in the hotel, of course, in which case she'd see him at dinner. Although, when she remembered the flick of those car keys and that metallic voice, maybe that was a pleasure she'd as soon miss out on.

Either way, she was hot, sweaty and tired after her long ride under the broiling mid-afternoon sun. And it hadn't helped, being put into this stuffy little den. There was probably a room like this in every Spanish hotel, she thought wryly, specially reserved for — shock, horror — young, unaccompanied English women riding motorbikes and wearing black leathers. Yes, Grant would have a lot to answer for when she finally met up with him in Marbella . . .

Now, though, every inch of her was crying out for that long, cool shower so, turning away, she went through to the tiny bathroom . . .

As soon as she opened the door again, she knew that someone was in her room. It was dark after the brightness of the shower-cubicle, so that the bedroom was in any case filled with shadows, but she halted abruptly, her hands tightening on the towel which she had been casually knotting under her arm.

Her eyes were still blurred from the shower, so was it imagination, or — her skin prickled — was that a darker shadow against the dark wood of the wardrobe? Surely not. She relaxed a fraction, then, above the smell of shampoo and soap from her own body, her nostrils caught the faint, sharp aroma of citrus from someone else's.

Her mouth filled with the acid taste of fear, so that she could not speak, let alone cry out. There was utter silence in the room, except that in the clammy darkness she could hear her own heart beating. And someone else breathing softly.

It was that soft, regular breathing which finally turned her fear to terror, and, her hand clutching on the towel, she plunged towards the door to the landing — and safety.

Only then did the shadow move. She glimpsed the pale gleam of a hand raised, saw it slicing towards her — but too late. Before she could even begin to draw in enough breath to scream, the world exploded around her in a pyrotechnic display of stars, then fizzled soundlessly into nothing as she plunged headlong into darkness . . .

★   ★   ★

The side of her neck — no, her whole head — was throbbing, as though a giant sledge-hammer were being rhythmically clanged inside her skull. From a long way off, Georgia heard someone groan, then realised it was herself and opened her eyes. While she was unconscious, the shutters had been half opened and she winced as the brilliant light hit her like another physical blow.

She was lying on her bed and now, lips clamped against the pain, she struggled to sit up. But her hand was caught behind her. Turning her head — very slowly, for the slightest effort threatened to make her temples burst — she saw that one wrist was pinioned with a leather strap to the metal bedstead.

She lay staring up at it in horrified disbelief. Was she having a nightmare? Would she wake in a moment, safe in her bed at home, and laugh at her overheated imaginings? But the pins and needles pricking down through her veins, the chafe of leather and metal buckle against the soft skin of her inner wrist — they were all too real.

With a little moan of fear, Georgia wrenched at her arm, then, as she writhed helplessly on the bed, she felt the coarse drag of the sheet against her skin. She was naked. Someone had laid her on the bed, shackled her to it and casually covered her with the sheet — and that someone was at this very moment coming back down the passage towards her room.

Her mouth dry with terror, she listened as the footsteps stopped, then she saw the door-handle turn and a man came into the room, walked over to where she lay and stood gazing down at her. He was between her and the window, so his face was in deep shadow, and beneath the flimsy sheet Georgia felt her whole body shrink. While she'd lain in that pit of darkness, had he . . . ?

'Wh-what do you want?' It came out as a croak.

From those shadowy features, there

was a gleam of pale eyes, but the man did not speak. As she turned her head in desperation, she caught sight of her leather shoulder-bag standing open on the dressing-table, her passport lying beside it. Nausea crawled through her. Oh, God, he was a thief, a common thief — and lying here, tied to the bed, her head spinning, she was powerless to stop him.

The man laughed softly. 'Do not alarm yourself, Señorita Leigh.' A harsh voice which rasped against her over-stretched nerves. 'I am not a sneak-thief. Your valuables are perfectly safe with me.'

In that case . . . All at once, naked beneath the sheet, she felt even more defenceless.

'Well, what do you want, then?' she asked hoarsely, all her other, darker fears flooding back.

She sensed rather than saw the thin smile. 'Not your body, either. I do not make a habit of violating unconscious young women.' He paused. 'And I am not in the habit of striking women, either.'

In spite of herself she gave a shaky laugh, then winced as a stiletto-blade of pain shot through her. 'Well, for a beginner you made a pretty good job of it. And I suppose you're also not in the habit of tying them up to the nearest bedstead?'

She tensed her arm but then, as the pins and needles shot down it again, she gave a barely suppressed whimper of pain. He leaned towards her, and as she flinched away she felt his fingers unbuckling the strap. Next moment her arm dropped limply on to the bed, the blood surging painfully back into it.

'A necessary expedient, while I spoke with Señora Morillo,' he said coolly. 'It would not have suited my plans if you had tried to run away from me.'

He was slotting the belt back into the waistband of — Georgia's eyes widened — cream sharkskin jodhpurs, topping a pair of black knee-high boots. As he sat on the bed, trapping the sheet between her hip and his thigh, his face came abruptly out of the shadow and her gaze rose reluctantly to it.

Lean, tanned, the jet-black hair combed smoothly back, eyes, beneath a screen of thick black lashes, the palest of winter greys, the nose aquiline, the mouth patrician, thin lips finely sculpted, but, she saw with another flicker of fear, with more than a hint of lurking cruelty. A face of immense male beauty, though the beauty was all but masked by the haughty pride — even arrogance — which was stamped on every feature.

Her eyes fell to the broad shoulders and muscled chest, straining against the black fine-knit polo shirt, and she thought suddenly, But of course, I should have guessed — the only possible face and torso to match up to those superb thighs and legs, glimpsed through the screen of scarlet bougain-villaea.

Even as her lips curved in a wry little

smile, though, another spasm of pain shot through her and she put up a hand to run her fingertips gingerly along the side of her neck. Her inner mouth was smarting too, and she winced as she tasted the salty tang of blood.

With a smothered exclamation, the man reached for her. Desperately Georgia tried to wriggle free but, catching her by the shoulders, he turned her back to him.

'*Calla*! Keep still,' he commanded, then began softly probing her flesh. 'Does that hurt?'

'No.' But her eyes had filled with tears of pain, and through the blur she saw his lips tighten momentarily.

'You are fortunate,' he said. 'There is nothing broken.'

'No — *you* are fortunate,' she snapped. Despite her fear and vulnerability, she mustn't be cowed by this man. 'You're lucky that I shan't be bringing an even more serious charge than common assault.'

'Common assault?' he responded

coldly. 'If I had chosen, I could have killed you with that blow, like a helpless rabbit. But your lip — you must have bitten on it as you fell.'

'Fell!' Her voice rose shrilly. 'That's one way of putting it.'

But he was already gently exploring her mouth with his fingertips. Instinctively she tried to turn her head away again, but he brought his other hand up, trapping her face against his palm. Her lip was stinging, yet through the smart she was all at once conscious of other, far more disturbing sensations whick flickered like summer lightning along every nerve-circuit to the furthermost corner of her body.

'Open wider.'

She wanted to say no, but under the hypnotic movement of those fingers — long, tanned, very strong, though the strength in them was not unleashed at the moment — she allowed him to pull down her lip. He was frowning as he looked at it, his face very near to hers, so close that his warm breath caressed her cheek and the potent mixture of citrus and male body enveloped her.

Then, quite without warning, the hooded eyelids lifted, the pale eyes looked straight into hers, and she saw herself reflected in his pupils — two tiny Georgias caught in the shining black. For a second longer their gazes locked and as she stared up at him she saw a look of surprise — no, total astonishment, even shock — flicker across his hard-planed features.

At that same instant something dark and menacing, something profoundly disturbing, seemed to emerge from the corners of the room and fill it with its frightening presence. Strange, terrifying emotions were washing through her so that she was drowning in a dark, tideless sea. A wave of dizziness all but engulfed her, and she knew that it was absolutely nothing to do with the blow which had been inflicted on her. Just for that fleeting second, something primeval had stirred in her and the stranger knew it — just as he would always know everything about her.

His gaze now, though, was remote as from his pocket he took a white handkerchief and shook out the crisp folds. Still holding down her lower lip, he began dabbing at the cut inside her mouth. The touch of his fingers was so delicate as to be almost imperceptible, and yet those strange sensations were swelling in her again, this time in a tide of heat which spread through her entire body.

She moved restlessly and he glanced directly at her — a cool, impersonal glance now. Whatever had briefly shaken his icy composure a moment before was now well back under control. The black, finely arched brows came down a fraction, then, 'I think the bleeding has stopped,' he said.

As he withdrew the handkerchief, she saw the tiny crimson circlets of blood. He looked down at them, gave a faint grimace, then thrust the handkerchief back into his pocket.

'Of course — ' there was a barely reined-in anger in his voice ' — you have only yourself to blame for this.'

'Oh, you mean I invited you to come bursting into my room and knock me out,' Georgia retorted, glad of the excuse to vent some of the turbulent feelings inside her.

'Any young woman who is foolish enough to ride unescorted — '

'Unescorted!'

'Dressed in a totally unfeminine manner — '

'You mean I should've been wearing a miniskirt and a low-cut blouse, I suppose.' She fingered her sore mouth gingerly, a defiant glint in her amber eyes. 'I happened to be riding a motorbike, so — '

'Precisely. Something that no self-respecting young woman ever should do.'

'Well, of all the — ' every short, coppery curl on Georgia's finely boned head quivered in outrage ' — arrogant, chauvinistic — '

'Chauvinistic? Not at all,' he said disdainfully. 'It is merely that I believe that a woman should be just that — a woman — and never run the risk of being mistaken for a man.'

And it seemed to Georgia that his eyes raked in undisguised contempt down her slender body, penetrating the flimsy sheet to remind himself — if he needed reminding — of the slim, boyish hips and the miserably small creamy shells of her breasts. She winced inwardly — she had been right; there *was* cruelty in that haughty face — but, too proud to let him see how his gibe had struck home, she stayed silent.

'Above all, none of this would have happened if you hadn't, for reasons best known to yourself, been impersonating your twin brother. I take it that you are Grant Leigh's twin?' the man went on as she gaped at him. 'The resemblance is quite remarkable.'

'Yes, we're twins,' she agreed mechanically, then blurted out, 'You know Grant?'

'Our paths have crossed,' he replied grimly.

'So,' she went on half to herself, 'you hit me because you thought I was Grant.'

'How gratifying that your injury has not dulled your mental capacities.'

'But — why?' In her bewilderment she was barely aware of his biting sarcasm. 'What has Grant ever done to you?'

Yes, what *had* he done? Grant, in his happy-go-lucky way, had been in some tricky scrapes in his time, but this was very different. However had he got on the wrong side of this dangerous man? And dangerous he was, very dangerous — every instinct was screaming a warning of that. A great deal of pent-up venom had gone into that blow . . . The icy fingers of terror, not for herself now but for Grant, brushed across the nape of her neck.

'What has he done? Oh, come now.'

The man's lip curled in open disbelief. 'Riding his highly distinctive motor-cycle, dressed in identical leathers, signing yourself in at the same hotel in the same manner — G. Leigh. Don't try to tell me that you and your brother are not extremely — close.'

Georgia did not at all care for the blatant sneer in his voice but, as she gathered herself to react, a chill thought struck her. 'They sent for you — from the hotel — didn't they?'

'Of course. The message reached me as I was about to set out riding.'

'So sorry to spoil your plans,' she muttered.

'They were under orders to inform me if he should ever be so ill-advised as to return.'

'Well, now you know that he hasn't come back. As you see, he isn't here.'

'No, but you are.' The cold grey eyes met hers, then without warning, he leaned forward, but as she flinched away he merely smoothed a tangled curl back from her brow. 'And the question is, what is to be done about it?'

'I'll tell you what's to be done,' she flung at him, hoping desperately that her defiance would mask the shiver that had flicked through her body at his touch. 'You're going to get out of my room — now. Otherwise I shall call the civil guard. There's one based in the village — I saw his office on my way here.'

'Ah, yes, Stefano,' he said easily, 'the son of my land agent. I think that, faced with two conflicting versions of the same event, he just might see things my way.'

'Oh, so you own the police here, as well as the hotel staff,' she muttered sullenly.

'I own this hotel, this village, this valley — everything and everybody in it.'

'You own . . . ?' She gave an unsteady laugh. 'You sound like some medieval overlord.'

'I couldn't have described my position better myself.'

'But this is the twentieth century, not the Middle Ages.' She shook her head in disbelief. 'And anyway, even if people pander to your inflated ego down here, I'm not one of your slaves. I'm a free, emancipated woman, and I — '

'Enough of this,' he cut in harshly. 'Where is your brother?'

'I — I don't know,' she whispered, all her pert defiance instantly gone. She'd been frightened when she'd thought he was a common thief. Now, gazing up at that angry face, sheer terror engulfed her.

'You were obviously on your way to meet him. Where is he?' He seized her by the shoulders, his hands digging into the bare flesh.

'Look — ' she ran the tip of her tongue round her swollen lip, barely aware now of the pain ' — you're quite wrong about whatever it is that you think Grant has done, so — '

'You have no address, no rendezvous written down among your possessions.' So that was what he'd been searching for in her bag. 'So it must be in your head.'

'You're mad, quite mad,' she said hotly. 'And if you think I'm going to help you get hold of Grant you couldn't be more wrong. Even if we did have a meeting fixed — which we haven't — you'd never get it out of me.' Under the sheet her hands were clenched tight. 'You — you could tear my toe-nails out one at a time, and I still wouldn't tell you.'

His grip clasped her like steel talons, and for a moment she thought he was going to try and shake what he wanted out of her, but then he abruptly released her.

'Get dressed.' He jerked his thumb at the chair where her underwear and black leather jacket and trousers lay. 'You are coming with me.'

'I am not — ' she began, but even as she clutched the sheet to her he ripped it away.

With a sob of terror she curled her naked body up into a tight ball but, seizing her arm, he jerked her upright. Another wave of dizziness went through her and she flung up her hands, so that they were splayed against his chest, and beneath the fine cotton of his shirt she could feel his powerful heartbeat.

When she looked up his features had blurred, then, as she shook her head to try and clear the grey fog that was enveloping her brain, she saw not one but four menacing faces bearing down on her. She tried to speak but her tongue had turned to wood, and as the faces shifted and shimmered a yawning chasm opened at her feet and she fell helplessly into its bottomless black vortex.

2

The hotel room was moving, bucketing over rutted ground, while beneath her the bed had turned into a cloud-soft expanse which exuded the smoky aroma of new leather.

Georgia half opened her eyes, tried to raise her head, then was forced to let it slump back as the dizziness spun gyrating circles in her brain again. She was still naked, still wrapped in the cotton sheet, a pillow wedged behind her head, but now she was sprawled on the rear seat of a car, which was hurtling along at a terrifying speed.

Turning her head just a fraction, she saw — what else but a familiar pair of broad shoulders under a black polo shirt, and a dark head, just one black half-curl marring the crisp edge as it curved into the nape?

Struggling upright, Georgia said in a

high, strained voice, 'Where are you taking me?' When there was no response, not a flicker, she punched her fist against his seat. 'I *demand* that you return me — at once — to the hotel.'

'It seems to me, Señorita Leigh — ' he was changing down, swerving to avoid something in the road ahead which she could not see ' — that you are in no position to demand anything.'

'You must be crazy if you think you can get away with this. I — I'll drag you through every court in Spain.' One shoulder lifted in a careless half-shrug, and she went on despairingly, 'I'm quite sure kidnapping is a serious offence here.'

'Ah, but I am not kidnapping you.'

'Not . . . ' She sat up straighter, clutching the sheet as it all but slipped away from her. 'What would you call it, then?'

'Oh, merely entertaining you as my guest for a while.'

For a while . . . She swallowed. 'And just how long do you intend to keep me?' In spite of herself, her voice shook.

'For as long as it is necessary, of course.'

And how long would that be? Until he broke her spirit and she told him what he wanted to know about Grant — and that was impossible, for they really did have no firm rendezvous arranged — or until he had achieved whatever else he had in mind for her? As she remembered that moment back in the hotel when he'd bent over her, when that dark force had uncoiled itself in the shadows, icy water seemed to trickle through her bowels, and she lay back, her fingers plucking at the sheet.

The car slowed and swung in through a pair of high, wrought-iron gates set in white walls, then they were plunged into the sombre green shade of a cypress avenue. They rounded a bend, and she just had time to glimpse high, stone walls rearing above them, then they drew up in an enclosed courtyard.

A second later her door opened and he was looming over her. 'Out.'

'No — no, I won't.'

She shrank away from him, scrabbling at the far door, but, his lips a thin razor-slash in his tanned face, he leaned across and scooped her into his arms. Impervious to the frantic kicks she aimed at him, he carried her in under an arched stone portico and, as they neared the huge, iron-studded door, it was opened by a grey-haired woman dressed in black. The man halted briefly and spoke a few curt words in Spanish.

'*Sí, Señor* Torres.' The woman nodded and hurried off down a passage, with no more than the briefest glance in her direction — for all the world, Georgia thought, as though half-naked young women being carried kicking and struggling over this door-step was a weekly occurrence. Maybe it was.

She had expected him to set her down now, but instead he crossed the spacious hall and began mounting the wide flight of marble stairs. What on earth was he going to do to her? This was remote Spain, not safe, suburban England. Was he going to exact some primitive revenge for this imagined crime of Grant's by raping his twin sister? Her heart almost bursting with terror, she fought like a wild thing until he was forced to a halt.

Only for an instant, though. Bracing himself against the wooden banister, he tightened his grip, crushing her to him, so that, locked against him, she could not move a muscle. As he continued up the stairs, she lay helpless as a tiny sparrow against his hard chest, and her breast rising and falling as she tried to gulp air into her lungs, all she could feel was his heart against her ribs. Her eye was on a level with his shirt — one of the little pearl buttons had been wrenched off, leaving a ragged hole. Hastily she averted her eyes, only to fasten them instead on the stern face, impassive save for the warning edge of colour along the cheekbones. Georgia stared at that dusky line. This was a man who wasn't used to anyone — and especially a woman — defying him. Defying him — so that is what you're doing, she thought, biting her lip to strangle the hysterical little sob.

There was a scratch on one cheek, though — from her nails, presumably. As it oozed a tiny pin-prick of blood the thought gave her no satisfaction, only added to her terror.

Along a wide passage, his heels clicking on the marble tiles, then he shouldered open a door, strode across the room and dropped her — fairly gently — on to a bed. As she lay spread-eagled, she saw that she had all but fought her way out of the sheet: her small breasts, a wide expanse of pale, creamy flesh, one thigh and long slender leg — all were exposed to the pale grey eyes.

With shaking hands she huddled herself under the sheet as he stood over her, hands on hips and breathing heavily.

'*Dios*! What a little hellcat you are.' He regarded her with loathing.

'I am when you're around,' she panted.

'But how I shall enjoy taming you.'

A cruel smile licked round the thin lips, but as she stared up at him, rigid with apprehension, there was a discreet tap at the door and the woman came in with a tray on which was a bowl and some cotton wool. She set it down beside the bed then, with one swift sidelong glance at Georgia, retreated.

He sat down on the bed, tore off a piece of cotton wool and dipped it into the water, which was clouded with antiseptic. Then, as she still lay looking up at him, like a hunted doe that, too tired to run further, just watched the tiger move in for the kill, he bent over her and gently stroked it across her aching neck. Patting the skin dry, he unscrewed a tube of ointment and smeared some on.

'This will take out the bruise.'

'Hope so,' she muttered ungraciously.

'It will, I promise you.' Was there a glint of dry humour in those pale eyes?

'It's a well-tried remedy — I use it on Leila, my thoroughbred mare, when she strains a fetlock. Now, open your mouth.'

As his fingers drew down her lower lip she closed her eyes, bracing herself not to show pain. But then, instead of stinging antiseptic, she felt the warmth of a pair of lips. Her eyes flew open and she tried to jerk her head away, but he trapped her face, tilting it so that she could not move.

As his lips brushed across the swollen split in her mouth she felt her breathing, which had only just calmed from her struggles, quicken again until she was panting softly. Then, as she felt not his lips but his tongue begin to lap the sore flesh, barely controllable sensations spiralled in her. Her hands fluttered up, the fingers tangling in his dark hair, and with a strange guttural sound she yielded her mouth to him.

When at last he withdrew his tongue she heard herself moan softly, then opened her eyes to see him regarding her with the narrow, feral smile of a predator certain of its prey. She gave an anguished gasp of humiliation, the colour stinging her skin far more painfully than the antiseptic had done, and jerked away from him.

He got to his feet, to stand looking down at her. 'Your bathroom is through there. I shall see you downstairs in fifteen minutes.'

'Dressed like this, I suppose?' she muttered and, unable to meet his gaze, gestured down at the crumpled sheet.

'Of course not.' A slight movement of his head indicated a fitted wardrobe of pale wood which ran the length of one wall. 'You will find something suitable in there.'

As he turned away, Georgia drew herself up. 'Now look here . . . '

At her tone, he swung back, that cleft between his haughty brows deepening visibly, and her pulses quickened. But, swallowing down her fear, she went on, 'I've got my own clothes, back at the hotel, so — '

'They will be brought here, together with your other belongings.'

'The motorbike!' She'd completely forgotten about that. If anything happened to it, Grant would never forgive her.

'*All* your possessions will be quite safe while you remain under my protection.'

'Your protection!' Her hand rose involuntarily to her still aching neck and, in spite of the sudden spark in his eye, she added stubbornly, 'Anyway, I want *my* clothes. If you think I'm wearing your mistress's cast-offs, you can think again.'

'And what makes you so certain that they belong to my mistress?'

His lips had tightened to that warning line again, but the imp of defiance inside her was still urging her on to self-destruction.

'Well, I'm sure no woman would ever be foolish enough to actually marry you. You're — you're a — '

But the ill-advised insult died in her

throat as, with a muttered oath, he seized her by the arms, finally dragging her up hard against his body to quell her as she fought against him once more.

'*Diablo!* Never in my life have I met a woman like you,' he ground out, his angry breath parting the curls on the crown of her head.

'Because I'm not a docile, well-trained slave, you mean?' She was panting again, not only because most of her breath had been squeezed out of her as he crushed her to him, but also because of the close proximity of every superb, masculine contour.

'Certainly 'docile' is not a word which could be applied to Señorita Georgia Leigh,' he said grimly. 'But understand this — as long as you are under my roof you will dress in the way that pleases me.'

'I — '

'You will choose clothes from here and will put them on — unless you want me to put you into them — and you will be downstairs in fifteen minutes.'

And he released her so suddenly that she staggered back a pace. The sheet was slipping again and, glowering at him, she tugged it up.

'I'm sorry, Señor Torres, but it's quite obvious that all the women who've had the misfortune to meet you have given you entirely the wrong idea.'

'No — they have given me the correct one,' he replied coldly. 'The knowledge that women are born to be subservient, obedient to their men — unless, of course, they are corrupted by dissolute individuals like your brother.'

'Grant?' Georgia gaped at him, aghast. Surely her brother hadn't been foolish enough to seduce this man's mistress — wife — any woman that he considered his personal property?

He nodded grimly. 'Precisely. And that is why I intend to track him down — with your help.'

'I've told you — never!'

She received a thin slash of a smile. 'Never is a long time, *querida*.'

'And if I refuse — what will you do? Take out your lust for vengeance on me, I suppose.' In spite of her defiant words, the hairs on the nape of her neck prickled.

'I have not yet made up my mind.' He studied her rumpled curls and flushed face for a few moments, his pale eyes hooded. 'The possibilities, after all, are endless.' His voice dropped to the purr of a sleek tiger. 'But I know I shall enjoy finding out.'

He glanced down at the slim gold watch at his wrist. 'Thirteen minutes.' And, swinging on his heel, he walked out.

As the door closed Georgia leaned against the wall, violent tremors shaking her slender frame, and when she put her hands up to her face she found that they were trembling. Whatever had possessed her to provoke such a man? He said he'd never met anyone like her

— well, she'd certainly never encountered a man remotely like him. Beneath the civilised veneer — the expensive car, the immaculate tailoring — there lurked a dangerous, unpredictable savagery. If she went on rousing his anger like this, what might he do to her, alone and defenceless as she was? And to react as she had done, melting at his touch, hanging in his arms, greedy for his mouth and lips . . . that could only have made him despise her even more, convinced him that she'd be powerless to resist whatever he chose to inflict on her.

The pretty little gilt and china clock on the mantelshelf tinkled. If she wasn't dressed and down on time, he'd no doubt be up here within seconds to drag her downstairs dressed just in the sheet — or less.

Her eyes widened at the opulence of the bathroom, all brown and cream marble, gold fittings and recessed spotlights. She stood in the doorway surveying it, then quickly showered and, taking a fluffy cream towel from a pile in an alcove, blotted herself dry, gazing into the full-length mirror.

A very pale Georgia stared out of the glass. Her heart-shaped face, with its straight little nose and slightly too wide mouth, normally the tone of a creamy magnolia petal, was drained of every vestige of colour, bringing her copper curls and large, golden-amber eyes into sharp relief. She was deathly pale — except along the side of her neck, where the bruise was a faint bluish tinge.

Her gaze travelled down, taking in, with the usual reluctance, her too slender figure. Georgia smiled ruefully, remembering the pocket-money she'd wasted on useless 'increase your bust by inches' miracle creams, the winter mornings when she'd shivered in the shower, gritting her teeth against the pain of a jet of icy water directed against her chest. She must have been — what? Seventeen? — when she'd finally come to terms with the fact that she and Rosie Jones, her voluptuously endowed best friend, had been constructed on entirely different assembly lines.

Back in the bedroom, Georgia stole a moment to look around her. The room was very prettily furnished — and with no expense spared. Her trained eye saw that, even as she was registering the pale wood, and the soft willow-green of the velvety carpet, which subtly echoed the green and rose of the curtains and bedspread. A bit too chintzy and frilly for her taste, but the overall effect against the sombre wood panelling and heavy plasterwork ceiling was very feminine.

And very expensive. When she'd left school, Georgia, intent on carving out a career which would make her independent, had thought about studying interior design before finally opting for landscape architecture. Her eye, though, was quite developed enough to spot a room which oozed wealth, and she hadn't been kicking and throwing futile punches so hard that she had not taken in, almost automatically, the superb pieces of antique furniture and porcelain down in the hall as she was being carried past them.

Who was he — this arrogant, terrifying man, who led a life of modern opulence yet behaved like an eighteenth-century brigand . . . ?

But on the china face of the clock the minutes were ticking away, and she hastily slid open the wardrobe door. The entire length was crammed with clothes, and beneath them was every sort of footwear from dainty sandals to a dozen pairs of beautifully made leather boots. She pulled out a stunning pair in palest cream, hand-stitched, with a fine gilt chain at the ankle and as her thumb caressed the soft leather, for the first time in her life she felt a little spasm of envy for the world's wealthy.

Straightening up, she began riffling through the clothes. It was difficult — the owner of those wonderful boots had clearly been built along Rosie Jones

40

lines — a head shorter than Georgia and well-rounded. And pink was obviously her favourite colour, a shade which did not at all suit Georgia's hair, while the style of most of the clothes was younger, more frivolous than she liked. Señor Torres clearly favoured youth, whether it was in a mistress or a child-bride. But then, he would, wouldn't he? Young, malleable, eager to be moulded to his exact requirements.

She had to wear something, though, so finally she picked out a white linen skirt which, slung low on her hips, would reach almost to her knees, and a shirt in soft turquoise silk. A chest of drawers was crammed with lingerie; one glance at the pretty cotton bras told her they were far too big, but she snatched up a pair of minute white panties.

As she slipped into them, however, for some reason the idea of the young girl who owned them jarred on her unpleasantly — almost, ludicrous as it was, as if she was jealous of this unknown woman. But, thrusting the thought away, she stepped quickly into the skirt. She buttoned the shirt then, tying a jade silk scarf round her hips, pulled the shirt out so that it hung in loose folds, disguising, she fervently hoped, the fact that beneath it she was naked.

She was running her fingers through her tousled curls when she heard a vehicle labouring up the drive. This room was at a corner of the building and a huge tree was growing just outside, but by kneeling up on the wide stone window-seat and peering through the gnarled branches she could see the vehicle as it passed beneath the window. It was an open truck and perched in it were her travel-bag, leather shoulder-bag and, looking faintly incongruous, the Rudge-Whitworth, its black and chrome body gleaming in the late afternoon sun.

As the truck disappeared round the corner of what looked like a stable block, the clock chimed again. Two minutes, and he'd be back up here to haul her out. All the shoes were quite impossible for her slender feet so, barefoot, she went out into the passage, where a young maid was obviously waiting. The girl bobbed a little bow then rather timidly gestured her to come and Georgia, with a reassuring smile totally at odds with her own nervousness, allowed herself to be escorted back down the wide staircase, across the hall and down another sombre passage.

The maid tapped at a door. '*Entra.*' Torres's voice was crisp and authoritative, and she scuttled off back along the passage, leaving Georgia to push open the door. He was sitting behind a huge desk, a pile of papers in front of him, but when she appeared he put down his pen and sat back, slowly swivelling the black leather chair and watching her over steepled fingers.

It seemed to her that never in her life had she made a longer journey than across that deep-piled cream carpet, under the scrutiny of those pale, unreadable eyes. When she halted in front of the desk he continued to regard her in silence, before finally glancing at his watch.

'Punctual to the second, Señorita Leigh.'

3

'Well, I'd hardly dare be otherwise, would I?' Georgia's inner tension added a sharp edge to the words.

One corner of his mouth flicked for a moment, but all he said was, 'You're learning fast, *querida*. Please sit down.'

There was a cream leather chair on her side of the desk, much lower than his — deliberately arranged, no doubt, so that she was forced to look up at him. To give herself thinking time, she glanced around the room. It was obviously an office — three telephones stood on the desk, while a laptop computer and fax machine were placed on a table alongside a steel filing cabinet. Of course — Torres had chosen to have her brought here to make clear that this was no social occasion.

'I rather thought that Isabel's clothes would be an improvement on that sheet you are so devoted to.'

Georgia's eyes jerked back to him and, conscious of his sardonic gaze, fixed — or so it seemed — on the faint outline of her breasts beneath the soft folds of turquoise silk, she shrank back slightly into the chair.

'Isabel? Is she . . . ?'

'My niece.'

'And she's away just now?'

'Thanks to your brother — yes.'

At the sudden savagery in his voice, she recoiled even deeper into her chair, but then as his words sank home she asked hesitantly, 'You mean, you think that she's run off with Grant?'

'I don't think, I know. The last sight of her, four weeks ago, was riding out of the village heading towards Málaga on the back of your brother's motorcycle.'

She stared at him aghast. Had Grant really been so foolhardy as to get himself involved with a girl from this man's family?

'If you were so sure of that,' she said

stoutly, 'why didn't you chase after her?'

'I was away on business in Madrid and by the time I returned the trail had gone cold. There has been no sight or sound of her since then.'

'Look, Señor Torres — ' Georgia leaned forward earnestly ' — obviously you're worried about your niece, but I'm quite certain you're mistaken about Grant. Even if he did give her a lift, I'm sure that's as far as it went. How old is she?'

'Sixteen.'

'Well, that proves it, then. Grant would never get mixed up with a sixteen-year-old. He's nine years older, and he's not a cradle-snatcher.' And at the chill, disbelieving laugh she added vehemently, 'It's far more likely that she's run off with some lad of her own age. Did she have any boyfriends?'

'There was one totally unsuitable youth some time ago, but I sent him packing.'

I bet you did, Georgia thought, and

you enjoyed every minute of it too.

'But what's it got to do with you, anyway?' she demanded. 'You're just her uncle — surely it's up to her parents to make her toe the Torres line?'

'My brother and his wife are both dead. I have been Isabel's guardian since she was two years old.'

'I see.' The sudden bleakness in his tone disconcerted her for a moment, and she went on more quietly, 'I'm sure you've got it wrong about Grant, really I am. It's true, he was in Spain a month ago, but by that time he can't have been heading for Málaga. He'd have been going north for the Santander ferry by then — which is presumably why you couldn't trace him.'

'Very probably. But he was cunning enough to lay a false trail south before doubling back.'

'No, it's not true.' She banged her clenched hands on the arms of her chair in frustration. 'Maybe your niece did hitch a lift from him — I'll give you that much. But it's much more likely that she was meeting with that boy-friend of hers. They'll have arranged some rendezvous outside the village and gone off together before you even knew she was missing. Yes, that's a much more likely explanation,' she wound up triumphantly, but when she looked up his eyes were like slivers of steel.

'Such loyalty — how very touching,' he sneered. 'But I am sorry to tell you that that young man has of course been closely questioned and eliminated from my enquiries. In any case, he would never have dared cross me again.' A smile flickered across those thin lips. 'No, it could only be an outsider, a foreigner, who would be so unwise as to tangle with me.'

'Look,' she said desperately, 'Grant and I, we're very close. We have been ever since — '

She broke off, biting her lip. She wasn't going to tell this man anything more than she had to — certainly nothing of the years of unhappiness she and her twin had endured during their parents' stormy marriage, or of the even greater pain of rejection when, after the divorce, their mother had remarried and they had been so obviously second-best to her new family — of the shared unhappiness and pain which had welded the bonds of fierce protective-ness each felt for the other.

Conscious of his eyes watching her, searching out the slightest betrayal of weakness, she continued, 'We don't have any secrets from each other, Grant and I. If he really had been so stupid as to run off with a sixteen-year-old Spanish girl, he'd have told me. Besides, he wouldn't have just abandoned her, and he certainly didn't bring her back with him to the flat we share in London.'

'Which is where he is now?'

'No.'

'So he is back in Spain.'

'I didn't say that,' she muttered.

'You did not need to,' he responded silkily. 'You are riding his motorcycle down to him. That is the truth, isn't it?'

'No. I mean — Oh, all right.' She expelled a long breath. This man, relentless in his pursuit of her brother, was bound to catch up with him eventually. But surely even he, sooner or later, would have to accept Grant's innocence, so really the quicker this whole business was sorted out the better. 'It's true, I am delivering the bike to him. He flew down to Marbella a couple of weeks ago to take up a crewing job on a charter yacht.'

'Its name?' Torres put in softly.

'I don't know, damn you,' she replied between her teeth. 'But right now it's somewhere in the Mediterranean — or halfway to the Azores, for all I know. I'm not due to meet up with Grant for a couple of weeks, and even then we've got no definite meeting fixed.'

'See you round the harbour, Georgie' — that was as near to an arrangement as her easygoing twin had come to making.

'So you have already informed me.'

Pushing back his chair, he uncoiled himself and, as she tensed in sudden apprehension, he came round to her side of the desk. He leaned against it, legs crossed, the toe of one polished boot casually brushing against her bare calf. He was doing it deliberately, she was certain — another of his ploys to unnerve her. But that didn't make it any easier to subdue the shivers — half-fear, half-excitement — which had all at once begun to course through her body.

'And why is your brother so anxious to have this ancient motorcycle brought to him?'

'Well, maybe you don't know much about vintage bikes . . . ' she began, and he raised one ever-so-slightly bored eyebrow.

'I'm sure you can enlighten me.'

'It's a 1929 Rudge-Whitworth — a collector's item, quite valuable. Grant found it rusting in a scrapyard and spent last winter doing it up in his spare time. And now someone he met down in Marbella has made him a marvellous offer for it, so he rang and asked me to bring it down to him.'

'Subjecting his sister to all the rigours and dangers of riding alone through Spain,' he sneered.

'There wasn't any danger — at least, not till I met you,' she retorted. 'Besides, I'm used to riding a motorbike. It's the best way of getting around London these days.'

'You work in London?'

'Some of the time.'

'Doing what?'

She shrugged. 'Oh, this and that.' Let him make of that what he liked. She didn't intend telling him one iota more about herself than she had to. Knowledge was power — that was what they said, wasn't it? — and she was more than enough in this man's power already. 'A job I had lined up fell through so I've come earlier than planned — I'd been turning it into a holiday.' Till I met you, was the unspoken rider this time. 'I haven't really had one for . . . '

Her voice tailed away. The toe was still swinging nonchalantly back and forth and the movement, slight as it was, was tensing the muscles which ran up his leg and into his thigh. Her eye traced them as they rhythmically tautened then relaxed in a mesmerising pattern. The blood was singing in her ears, and when she wrenched her gaze upwards he was looking straight at her. Their eyes locked, the air hummed, vibrating round them like softly plucked violin strings, then she blundered to her feet.

'I . . . ' Her mouth was dry as tinder. 'It's very hot in here. Can we go outside?'

'But of course.'

He came to his feet, the urbane host, and, crossing to the far end of the room, pushed open the glass doors and gestured her past. Outside was a paved terrace and beyond that a small garden, surrounded on three sides by stone walls. Hearing Torres just behind her,

Georgia hurriedly took a step on to one of the narrow gravelled paths which led to the centre, where she glimpsed a fountain. But she had forgotten that her feet were bare, and pulled up with a little gasp of pain as she trod on a sharp flint.

Next moment, she had been caught up in his arms and was being carried along the path, her toes brushing softly against the tangle of climbing jasmine so that they released its perfume. But far more intoxicating than those sweet, white, star-like flowers was the sharp tang of citrus combining with the musky, vibrant aroma of a male body.

She lay clasped against his chest, feeling the scent permeate her skin until, like some powerful drug, it seemed to enter her blood, thickening it so that it ran turgidly in her veins as her entire body became enveloped in a cloying heat.

At the very centre of the garden there was a circular pool, and when he set her down her legs were so weak that she swayed before sinking down on to the low marble parapet. Her face averted to hide its hectic colour, she trailed her fingers in the water, grateful for the shock of its icy chill.

'It is cold always, because it comes from a spring deep in the rocks.'

'I see.'

She stared down at the tiny wavelets her fingers were making among the water-lilies, then allowed her gaze to move across the surface in which she saw herself reflected and, just behind her, Torres. Their eyes met in the water for a long moment until, as her hand jerked, their faces rippled and disappeared.

'The spring was the reason, I imagine, why my ancestor built the castle here — to ensure a water supply in times of danger.'

The castle? But of course; she should have realised earlier. Those soaring walls, glimpsed as he'd carried her from the courtyard, the massive interior walls, barely softened by the dark wood panelling — and now that she looked up beyond the garden she saw jagged crenellations outlined against the still cloudless sky.

'And when he married,' Torres continued, 'it is said that he had this garden laid out for his wife to spend the long hot afternoons here.'

Georgia looked around her, taking in for the first time the intricate pattern of the garden. This pool, with its central fountain and tiny jets playing around the brim, the gravelled walks, lined with low hedges, narrow water channels running into stone basins, an arcaded walk of white plaster arches along one end, narrow cypress trees, like dark green fingers, mirrored in the clear water — these were the formal elements, the bones of the garden, which her professional eye registered immediately. And on the sculptured bones was the flesh — sprawling bougainvillaea, roses and jasmine, clipped bay trees in terracotta pots, orange trees, their ripe fruit glowing among the glossy leaves.

'It's very beautiful,' she said slowly. 'Surely, though, it's a Moorish rather than a Spanish garden?'

'You know about such things?'

'A little,' she replied evasively.

'You are quite right.' His vouce was bland, but something in his tone made her swing round to him. 'Yes, Señorita Leigh — ' his grey eyes subtly mocked her ' — I am of Moorish blood — or, rather, part-Spanish, part-Moorish.'

Of course. Georgia forced herself to meet his ironic gaze. That arrogance, the aquiline nose, the cruelty lurking in the thin lips. And, above all, his attitude to her — a mere female who had yet to be taught her natural role of unquestioning subservience to the male.

As the apprehension stirred in her again, she bent to sniff the golden heart of a white rose. 'But I thought all the Moors were driven out of Spain centuries ago.'

'Not my ancestor.' When she glanced up from beneath her lashes, there was a narrow smile on his face. 'He was, I think, a great survivor. He had fallen in love with Spain, married the daughter of a Spanish nobleman, and no one could be permitted to force him out.'

'I can imagine,' Georgia put in drily, more to herself than him, and heard his wry laugh.

'True, he had to abandon his lands around here for a while and retreat to the coast, but not one step further.'

'You amaze me.' Georgia took a final deep sniff of the honey-scented flower, then met his eye innocently. 'And what did he do then? Took up needlework, I suppose.'

Her pulse-beat quickened instantly. This was a dangerous game, baiting a tiger.

'No,' he returned levelly. 'He came back here as soon as he could, rebuilt this place — and of course this garden. Gardens, Señorita Leigh, have always been important to us — perhaps because our original homeland was a bleak desert under pitiless skies. But, whatever the reason, we have always created gardens. On a searing afternoon, to have cool shade, the soft splash of water, the scent of flowers . . . Keep still.' As she flinched away he cupped her face in steel fingers, holding her while he snapped off a white rose and tucked it into the curls behind her ear. 'And most important, of course, a beautiful woman to enjoy . . . ' He paused, then, as his eyes locked with hers, went on suavely, 'It with. What could be more perfect, do you imagine?'

She tore her eyes free, an almost physical wrench. 'I — I don't know. Look, Señor Torres — '

'Please.' He grimaced. 'My name is Ramón.'

'No, I'd rather — '

'And I shall call you Georgia. Georgia.' He said it again, this time as though he were tasting it, savouring it, and a strange, erotic *frisson* shimmered through her. He was still holding her face and the heat from his fingers was burning into her flesh, so that when he at last released her she involuntarily put up a hand to rub it. What was happening to her? she asked herself despairingly. She was a tough — at least, seemingly tough — and independent, self-reliant woman, yet she could feel her will being insidiously drained away, so that all the time she was waiting, in fear and trembling, for him to make the next move.

'Was . . . ' She cleared her throat and began again. 'Was it you who modernised the castle?'

'My grandfather began the work, my father carried it on, and I have completed it.'

'But I bet you've kept the dungeons and torture chambers — in full working order.' Maybe a pert provocativeness was the best way to deal with this man. He obviously wasn't used to that in a mere woman.

'Of course.'

'I'm surprised you didn't lock your

niece down there and feed her on bread and water.'

'If I had known what she and your brother were planning, I would have flung them both down there.'

Her eyes flew to his face again. There was no hint of humour there — he was deadly serious.

'But I've told you,' she began. 'Grant — '

'Your brother is unimportant, a nothing,' he broke in curtly, 'but Isabel is an innocent, sheltered girl. Young for her age, headstrong — exactly like her mother.'

Without warning, the hard edge had gone from his voice, and the harsh lines of his face had softened too, into a tender smile. But as Georgia stared at him he caught her eye and that amazing tenderness was gone like a dream.

His lips twisted. 'Yes, you are right. I loved Luisa. We were very young but unofficially engaged. Then, when my older brother returned from abroad, she fell headlong in love with him, broke our engagement and they were married within a month.'

And she broke more than the engagement, Georgia thought suddenly, for she had glimpsed pain in his eyes. While she was about it, she broke your heart too. Her own tender heart ached for the tough man beside her who, as if determined to show no more weakness, had thrust his hands into his pockets and was leaning against the trunk of an acacia tree.

'And what happened to them?' she asked tentatively.

He shrugged. 'They were killed in a powerboat accident.'

'And Isabel — does she look like her mother?'

'Yes, but the main resemblance is personality — that same streak of wilfulness, wildness even, which I have tried to subdue.'

'You mean — ' she gave him a tremulous smile ' — you tried to break her spirit. Oh, don't get me wrong,' she added, as his eyes narrowed to angry slits, 'you did it, I'm sure, with the best of motives — but you were wrong.'

'You think so?'

His voice was sharp, but she went on vehemently, 'I know so. If you try to alter someone's personality, put them in a strait-jacket, it's — it's *dangerous*.'

'You know nothing of Isabel.'

'No, but — '

'So do not speak of her. You and she — you are light-years apart.'

'Well, thanks,' she replied ironically. 'All compliments gratefully received.'

'Isabel is a young, naïve girl, while you, by your own admission, are a free, emancipated woman — with no doubt the sexual experience to match.'

If only he knew! But even as the humiliating colour flooded her cheeks Georgia bit back the response and instead went on, 'But can't you see that by being, well, over-protective you just might have made her rebel? Any young girl of spirit — '

'Isabel was totally obedient to my

wishes — until she was corrupted by your brother.'

'No — no, you're wrong!' she exclaimed despairingly. 'Look, Señor — ' And as the dark brows came down, 'All right — Ramón. Let me go on to Marbella. As soon as I find Grant, I'll persuade him to come back here and he'll convince you of his innocence, I'm sure he will.'

His lips twisted in a mirthless smile. 'You seriously expect me to release you? This would be the last place on earth you or your precious brother would come to, were I so foolish as to set you free.'

'But I give you my word that we'll come back.' Her voice shook with the need to persuade him. 'Grant might even be able to tell you what her plans were — who she met — where she is now, even.'

She looked up at him imploringly, but his face was implacable. 'No. You will remain here with me, to act as bait.'

'Bait? I — I don't understand.'

'When you do not arrive in Marbella, he will come looking. He clearly cares deeply for that so-valuable motorcycle of his, whatever he might feel for you, and he will follow its trail until he reaches here.'

'But I've told you, he's not expecting me yet. It could be three weeks or more before he even starts to search for me.'

'So much the better.'

Something in his tone jerked her eyes to him. 'Wh-what do you mean?' she faltered.

'Simply that while we are waiting the time can be passed — enjoyably, by both of us.'

Just for a moment there was a silence, so profound that it seemed to fill not just the small garden but the whole world. But then, as the birdsong, the soft tinkle of fountains returned, Georgia said tautly, 'Correct me if I'm wrong, but are you suggesting an affair?'

He shrugged. 'If you wish to put it

that way. A pleasurable diversion is how I would prefer to describe it.'

His pale eyes held hers in a challenging gaze, a fluttering moth on the end of a pin, but then she burst out, 'Just how hypocritical can you get? Here you are, foaming at the mouth because you think Grant has seduced your precious ward, and — '

'Seduced,' he cut in. 'Precisely. But in our case seduction, I am sure, will not be necessary.'

'It would have to be rape, then!' she exclaimed furiously. 'That's the only possible way you could ever — '

'Oh, Georgia.' His voice caressed her like a physical touch, so that, horrified, she felt her body stir into life under the husky timbre. 'There will be nothing so crude as rape between us. You cannot deny the attraction — it has been there from the very beginning.'

She knew it — she too had felt it, the air between them shimmering, her body growing warm and languorous under the potency of his spell. Never in her life before had she experienced feelings like this for any man, yet some deep, ancient female instinct warned her just how vulnerable she was, how easy it would be to succumb. And she couldn't hide her weakness from him — he knew her through and through. That was the danger of the man — but she had to fight him, or be lost forever.

'From the very beginning? Tell me, does that mean before or after you knocked me out?' she enquired ultra-sweetly.

'Be quiet.'

But he was not angry this time as, lifting his hand, he began to run one fingertip round her full lips. Georgia felt herself sway towards him. Her blood lay heavy in her veins, her breathing had all but stopped, and for a terrifying second she thought that she would faint. But even as her eyelids fluttered down she fought her way back to consciousness and drew in a shuddering, life-reviving breath.

'How can you talk about an affair?'

she demanded. 'You don't even like me — you despise me.'

He gave a faint grimace. 'I have not said that. True, I do not approve of your casual lifestyle, but you intrigue me like no other woman I have ever met.'

'But I don't set out to,' she replied in bewilderment.

'And that, *querida* — ' he gave her a crooked little smile ' — is precisely why you attract me so. With your cropped hair — ' he rested his hand on the crown of her head, his fingers lightly caressing her curls ' — and unbecoming clothes, you appear to be making one statement to the world: that you wish to deny your womanhood. But your body, all long, slender curves, your eyes, and what I glimpse in them, those tremulous lips that beg to be kissed — all this tells me something very different.'

'Oh, how ridiculous — ' she began, but he overrode her feeble protest.

'It tells me there is a passionate femininity beating within you. And that is what I intend to search out.'

His hand moved down, his thumb gently stroking her neck, very slowly, so that the tiny hairs stirred one by one.

'Oh, Georgia.' His voice had dropped to a soft, insidious purr. 'In the intimacy of my bedroom, in the seclusion of this garden, I shall hear you cry out with abandon, writhe in ecstasy in my arms — '

'No. Never!' With a desperate effort, she wrenched herself free. 'Never, I tell you!'

And, heedless now of the sharp gravel stabbing at her feet like daggers, she ran headlong down the path.

4

Back in her room Georgia flung herself on the bed, shaking uncontrollably in every limb. After she didn't know how long there was a knock at the door. She went rigid, but only the young maid came in, with a tray which she set down beside the bed.

Georgia lay where she was, one arm shielding her face until the door closed again. She thought she caught the soft click of a key turning, and when she finally roused herself to cross to the door, her footsteps silent on the dense carpet, it would not open. Her eyes blank with fear, she went back to the bed and sat on the extreme edge, hugging her arms to her chest.

There was a pot of tea on the tray, and a plate of small almond cakes. She couldn't eat — her throat was so tight that a single mouthful would have choked her — but maybe a cup of tea would revive her, even calm those butterflies of panic which were fluttering crazily in her stomach.

As she set down the teapot, she caught sight of herself in the dressing-table mirror, her hair a halo of glossy fire around a deathly pale face which somehow seemed to have shrunk, making the eyes seem even more wide and staring.

What was she going to do? She was trapped here, as a lure for Grant — for as long as it took. That was what Ramón Torres had said, wasn't it? And he calmly intended making her his sexual plaything while he waited. 'Let me go on to Marbella.' She could hear herself saying it, and felt a small, hysterical laugh well in her at her own naïveté. 'Let me go,' when she was in the power of a man who, once he had set his pitiless hand on anything — anyone — would never release it.

Torres. He was not remotely like any other man she had ever encountered.

72

Spanish-Moorish, a potent, lethal mixture — the suave, cultivated westerner, and contained in the same silky brown skin, the barbarian, the ruthless plunderer with that streak of cruelty which made her afraid of what she sometimes glimpsed in those opalescent eyes.

Somehow she had to reach Grant — but not to bring him here. Torres could never be persuaded of his innocence, and anyway, if she could once get away, no power on earth would ever entice her back here again.

Unable to sit still a moment longer, she pushed her tea away untasted and as she leapt to her feet she saw for the first time that her luggage had been placed in the corner, beside the wardrobe. Money, passport, even the motorbike's ignition key — they were all still there in her bag. Torres obviously saw no risk of her escaping — or maybe he thought she simply wouldn't dare.

But if only she could get out of this room. On the dressing-table was a silver box of hairpins and pretty, brightly coloured clips. It was supposed to be easy to pick a lock, wasn't it? Taking one of the pins, she knelt on the carpet by the door and, poking in the ends, tried to fasten them on the key. After twenty fruitless attempts, though, all she succeeded in doing was knocking it out so that it fell with a little clatter on to the marble tiles outside, and she leaned her forehead against the panel, tears of angry frustration blurring her eyes.

Georgia was hauling herself wearily to her feet, when she heard a soft scrabbling noise and, swinging round, saw the branch sway softly against the glass again. For a moment she stared at it, then flew across the room, scrambled on to the window-seat and flung open the window. She leaned out, measuring the sheer drop in the dusk, then sat back on her heels, feeling slightly sick. She'd climbed trees often enough when she was a child, spurred on by the fierce need to do everything at least as well as her brother. But she'd never climbed an old, gnarled tree, starting at the top where the branches, although they looked strong enough, could be rotten right through for all she knew.

But, rotten or not, this was her only chance of escape. She swallowed down that queasy sensation then, wriggling off the seat, quickly stripped off the borrowed skirt and top and, in feverish haste now, hauled herself into her leathers, then pulled on her trainers, barely noticing how her fingers shook as she tied the laces.

She couldn't take her case, of course, but, slinging her bag across one shoulder, she climbed back on to the window-seat and peered down just once more. Well, if she fell, at least she wouldn't have to worry about Ramón Torres, or anything else, for quite some time. Her lips twisted at the grim gallows humour then, taking a deep breath to steady her racing heartbeat, she eased herself out on to the branch.

After the ten longest minutes in her

life she stood, scratched and shaky-legged but triumphant, at the foot of the tree. She patted its warm, solid trunk in a gesture of thanks, then began making her way towards the rear of the castle, where she had seen the motor-bike being taken.

Nerve-crunching moments later she was in a cobbled stable-yard, one end of which had clearly been converted into garages. It was almost dark now and like a shadow she flitted across to the first door. She opened it a crack and saw the sleek grey shark — a Ferrari, she realised now — which had brought her here. The next garage held a Range Rover — and the third the Rudge-Whitworth.

Hardly daring to breathe, she wheeled it out and across the yard, under the curious gaze of three horses. One of them snorted softly to her and Georgia whispered, 'That's right, boy, you tell your master from me to go and jump in the lake.'

She stopped in the yard entrance, just

in the deep shadow before the light which shafted from a ground-floor window, then, not breathing at all now, settled herself astride the bike and put her foot on the kick-start — at the same instant that a horseman came cantering round the corner.

They saw each other simultaneously. Torres leapt from his horse just as, beyond coherent thought with terror, she kicked, and, for the first time ever, the Rudge-Whitworth let her down. She had no second chance; he pounced on her and dragged her bodily off the seat, sending the machine crashing to the ground.

'What the hell do you think you're doing?' he snarled.

His face was all but invisible in the darkness, but she felt the fury in him. From somewhere, though, she dredged up the courage to defy him.

'What does it look as if I'm doing? I'm leaving.'

She made a snatch at the handlebars but he seized her hand, and when she kicked him on the shin he muttered an oath, then, swinging her up over his shoulder, carried her round to the front entrance and into the hall.

Once inside, he let her slide down until she stood on her feet, her hair in wild disorder, her face scarlet from being hung upside-down and her amber eyes spitting fire. He himself was breathing heavily, his face flushed — though more, she guessed, from anger than exertion — and he had another scratch on his cheek to match the first. He held her by the wrist, his fingers digging into the soft flesh so that when she looked down she could see the bracelet of tiny bruises already springing up.

'*Diablo*. What a woman.' He shook his head as though in disbelief. 'How did you get out? Did María forget to — ?'

'No,' she broke in quickly as his features took on, if possible, an even more furious expression. 'She locked me in all right. I climbed down the tree.'

'You — you crazy little fool!' He shook her. 'You could have been killed.'

'Well, I wasn't, so what are you going to do about it?' she flung back at him, boldly enough, though inside she was hollow with the terror of what might have happened — and just what he would do with her now.

'If I put you in another room, will you give me your word that you will not try to get away again?'

'Certainly not. And you'd better chop down every tree within climbing distance, because I'll — '

'The trees have been growing here for two hundred years,' he ground out. 'I see no reason to fell them simply to keep in one undisciplined little hellcat.'

'In that case, you'd better put me in the dungeon, hadn't you?' She was goading him, laying herself open to terrible danger, but somehow the misery and fear in her — and anger that he should dare to treat her this way — was lashing her on. 'Lock me up and — and starve me into submission.'

He stood gazing down at her, a rather strange expression on his face, but then shrugged carelessly. 'As you will.'

Grabbing her by the wrist again, he began towing her along the passage, taking her to the very end then down a flight of stone steps and along another passage, cold and filled with shadows.

'Wh-where are you taking me?' she panted. 'You can't really — '

'Can't I?' he replied grimly and, pushing open a heavy, studded door, he clicked down a switch then thrust her through ahead of him.

Georgia, eyes dilating with shock, stared around the enormous, low-ceilinged room. She licked her ashen lips, then swung round on him. 'Wh-what is this place?'

'The dungeon, of course — which you expressed such an ardent desire to be acquainted with. Or, to be more precise, the torture chamber.'

And, letting her eyes slide reluctantly past him, she saw instruments standing silently, as though awaiting their next victim: chains and fetters hanging from the walls, a rack, a tall black case which Georgia recognised as an iron maiden, and others which, after one horrified glance, she shuddered away from.

'How do you like it?' He looked down at her, a glint in his eyes.

'All right,' she said in an unsteady voice, 'you've made your point — so now take me back upstairs.'

'Oh, but there's no hurry, surely?' he replied lazily. 'For instance, while we are here, why don't we try the rack for size?'

Before she could move he had caught her up in his arms, swung her off her feet and set her down again, her back against the rack. He leaned towards her, his body pressing her backwards over the wooden table, his face coming down very near hers, his breath fanning her averted cheek.

'Do you like that, Georgia?' he murmured.

'No — please.' Her voice was shaking and he straightened up, though still keeping a firm hold on her wrist.

'So you have learned your lesson?'

'Wh-what lesson's that?' Desperately she tried to infuse an ounce more bravado into her voice.

'Never to defy me again.'

'Oh, that? Of course not.'

For a moment he regarded her flushed face, her small head set proudly on her slender neck, in silence, then said brusquely, 'Come.'

So he had tired of his cruel teasing. She turned towards the door, but instead he forced her to cross to the far wall, where the chains hung down.

'Now, take off those revolting clothes.'

'No. No, I won't, and you can't — Oh!'

The cry was torn from her as, without another word, he caught hold of the zip beneath her chin and, ripping it down, revealed her creamy skin and small, rounded breasts. She heard his breath hiss in his throat as, scarlet with shame, she flung her free arm across her chest, but then, his lips tightening, he wrenched the zip back up again.

Catching up one of the fetters, he clipped it over her wrist, the metal icy cold, and turned a key in the lock. He slipped the key into his pocket and stood looking at her, an odd little quirk at his mouth.

'Sleep well, *querida*.'

'Sleep? You mean — ' Georgia's voice rose shrilly ' — you're leaving me here all night? You can't.'

He gave an infinitesimal shrug of regret. 'But you see, as you have told me several times, I cannot trust you. And besides, I wish to teach you a sharp lesson. After a night down here you will not, I think, be quite so ready to defy me tomorrow. That is, of course, if the rats have left anything of that slender, delectable body for you to defy me with.'

Georgia all but threw herself down on the floor at his feet, promising anything — anything not to be left here alone in this terrifying place. But her stubborn pride somehow kept her upright and, with a casualness she had thought was beyond her, she merely glanced down at the gleaming metal chain.

'Rats or not, you certainly keep this place in good shape. It obviously gets plenty of use.'

His pale eyes glinted. 'Not exactly. I open the castle several times a year to the public, in aid of a local children's home. And of course — ' the ironic note in his voice deepened ' — what the peaceful, law-abiding citizens want to see above all are the dungeons and these instruments. So I keep them in pristine condition.'

'I see,' she muttered, but then, still driven by the urgent need not to be bested by him, added recklessly, 'But I bet you still make a habit of keeping young women chained up down here — just the sort of thing I'd expect from a sadist like you.'

His lips thinned. 'Not at all. You are privileged to be the first.'

'My goodness.' Georgia forced a light

laugh. 'This is turning out to be quite a day for you, isn't it? The first time you've ever knocked a woman out, and now you've put one in chains. Two firsts in one day! Congrat — '

'You know something, Señorita Leigh? You talk far too much. That wide, beautiful mouth of yours was made for something very different.'

And, before she could turn her head aside, his lips came down on hers, taking her mouth in a fierce kiss. When she tried to wrench away he merely put up his hands, tangling them in her curls, to hold her to him. Unable to escape, she tried desperately to ignore his tongue sliding in to make a conquest of her unwilling mouth, but the taste of him, the scent of him filling her nostrils — everything was conspiring to beg — no, imperiously demand a reaction from her, until, aghast at her own weakness, she sensed her treacherous body beginning to respond.

Her nipples hardened, thrust against the leather of her jacket, and she felt molten heat ignite her loins. With a little moan, half-despair, half-desire, she sagged against him, and only then did he draw back, holding her from him by the elbows. There was a faint line of colour along the hard-cut cheek-bones, and through his slightly parted lips she could see even white teeth.

'I will give you one final chance. Are you prepared to promise me that you will not try to escape?'

Her mouth was tingling, though less from the pain of assault than the feel of him, and her eyes dropped until they were screened by her lashes.

'No,' she replied in a low voice.

He put his thumb under her chin, tilting her face. A tear hung on her lashes and he delicately picked it off with the tip of his little finger, then dropped it on to his tongue. It was as if he was tasting it, and that same little erotic thrill which had run through her when he'd spoken her name rippled through her body again.

'So, *buenas noches*. Sleep well,

querida.' And, turning on his heel, he walked out, closing the door behind him.

This time there was no need for him to lock it and, looking down at the fetter round her wrist, Georgia grimaced ruefully. 'Well, my girl,' she said aloud, 'you took a chance. You thought he wouldn't like to be crossed — and now you know it.'

Her voice, very small, echoed softly around the room; she felt another tear trickle down her cheek and in the intense silence heard it plop on her jacket. There was a pile of sacks against the wall and, knees buckling, she sank down on to them, hugging her knees to her chest.

Oh, brother mine, she thought suddenly, with a tinge of bitterness, the things I do for you. Knocked out, kidnapped, and now locked in a dungeon.

No, don't blame Grant, an inner voice cut in sharply. It isn't his fault you're down here. You provoked Ramón

Torres into it, and you know exactly why you did that, too. You're so frightened of the man, of the effect he's having on you every time he looks at you, every time he touches you, that it's self-defence. He thinks you're so sophisticated, so sexually mature, that this affair he's so intent on will be just as meaningless to you as it is to him. He'd laugh if he knew the truth — that you just can't handle him because you're so totally inexperienced. So you take refuge in childish insults — they're your only weapon. You're terrified of him, yes, but you're even more terrified of yourself. And that's the truth, isn't it?

'No, no, it's not,' she moaned, then, hearing the words echo once more, laid her cheek on her knee and closed her eyes, rocking to and fro in misery until she drifted into a shallow sleep . . .

The sound of footsteps roused her. As the door opened she scrambled unsteadily to her feet and leaned against the wall for support as Ramón came in. He had changed — that was the first fact her exhausted brain registered. Now he was wearing a long-sleeved white shirt, dark blue tie and grey trousers. She watched as he kicked the door to behind him and came across to her, unwillingly taking in how the shirt set off his darkly saturnine features and the way the trousers hugged his lean yet powerful thighs.

He was carrying a silver tray which he set down on a wooden chest near her, then, hooking a stool across with his foot, he perched on it, studying her thoughtfully.

'So you have not been eaten by rats?'

'No.' She scowled at him. 'I frightened them away.'

'Hmm. Yes, I can imagine that you could be more than a match for a pack of rodents.'

A silver coffee-pot and matching cream-jug, a lovely old porcelain cup and saucer, a balloon glass of cognac and — Georgia almost salivated at the sight of it — a dish of pink and white sugar almonds stood on the tray. As she watched, he casually poured a cup of coffee, added a dash of cream and picked it up, swirling it so that the cream flowed in a luscious arc over the dark surface. The fragrance of the coffee drifted across to her, making her taste-buds respond. But she wouldn't accept it. When he offered it to her she'd refuse — or, better still, take it and fling it over that beautiful crisp white shirt.

But even as she braced herself he took a leisurely, savouring sip. Then, while she looked on in stunned disbelief, he set down the cup and, still seemingly oblivious of her, took a pink sugar almond from the dish with long, fastidious fingers. He was about to put it in his mouth when he caught her eye.

'Hungry?' There was a faint gleam in his own eyes.

'Well, bread and water wouldn't come amiss,' she muttered.

Tossing the almond back into the dish, he drained the cognac then uncoiled himself and came down on his haunches beside her. She drew back in alarm, her chain jangling, but he merely took the key from his trouser pocket and unlocked the metal bracelet. As she pulled her hand free, flexing the sore wrist, he hauled her to her feet.

'Come with me.'

To Georgia's weary eyes, the long flight of stone steps looked like a mountain range stretching away.

'Can you walk?' Ramón asked curtly, as if sensing the utter fatigue of her mind and body.

Summoning all the tattered remnants of strength, she replied, 'Of course I can.'

Halfway up, though, she stubbed her toe painfully against one of the stone steps. She bit hard on her lip to suppress the whimper of pain but, two steps higher, he must have heard, for he stopped, turned, then, seeing her face, muttered under his breath and came back down to her. Too exhausted to protest, she allowed herself to be lifted into his arms and carried up the rest of the flight.

This was the — what? — fifth time at least that he'd carried her today, she thought bemusedly. It was getting to be more than just a habit. But as the hysterical little giggle welled in her he shouldered open a door and set her down in what was obviously a dining-room, beautifully proportioned — Georgia's dazed senses just about registered that — with a long, polished table in the centre. Two silver candlesticks stood at one end, where a place was laid for one.

'Before you eat, change out of those appalling clothes. I have brought this downstairs for you.'

He caught up a black robe which lay across the back of a superb eighteenth-century chair, and tossed it at her.

Rose-pink staining her cheeks, she put one protective hand to the zip of her jacket. 'No, I'd rather — '

He scowled. 'You change — now. Or you don't eat.'

'I can see why Isabel ran off,' she

hurled at him. 'Y-you're a tyrant — a chauvinistic tyrant.'

'Very probably. Now — do you wish me to undress you?'

The memory of that fleeting expression as he had ripped open the jacket in the dungeon made the warm colour flood right through her.

'No, thank you,' she replied stiffly. 'I can manage.'

'As you wish.' Picking up a magazine, he sauntered off to the far end of the room and dropped into a chair, his back to her.

She stared at that back for a very long moment, but finally kicked off her trainers, peeled herself out of the jacket and trousers and snatched up the black robe. It was as soft and light as a cloud — cashmere, it had to be — and it smelled faintly of Ramón. It must be his. The thought of that superb male body wrapped in it, chest and legs bare, halted her for a second, the blood coursing a fraction faster through her veins. But then, as he loudly closed the magazine and leaned forward to set it on a low table, she hastily pulled on the robe.

She was tying the knot with slightly unsteady hands when he glanced over his shoulder, then went across to the huge stone fireplace — empty at this time of year, apart from an enormous arrangement of white lilies and gladioli — and pulled a bell-rope.

'Go and sit down.'

'But . . . ' Georgia hesitated, her eyes on the damask napkin, gleaming silver, beautiful Sèvres china. She was ravenous — had never been so hungry in her entire life — but somehow her befuddled brain strongly suspected that if she once ate a meal under this roof, well . . .

'I said sit down.'

His brows came down in a dark frown, just as the door opened and a maid appeared. She set down a tureen of soup and a basket of rolls and, with a mumbled, 'Thank you,' Georgia slid into her place. The soup — fresh vegetable — was delicious, as was the dish of slightly spiced beef in melting slices which followed, accompanied by a platter of baby vegetables.

As she ate she tried unsuccessfully to ignore Ramón Torres. Just beyond the circle of light from the candles, he was lounging in an armchair near the fireplace, his long legs stretched out in front of him. Every time she glanced fleetingly in his direction he was watching her, his eyes narrowed to pale slits. He looked like a sleek yet sleepy cat, but she was not fooled for an instant. If she dared to try anything, that misleading air of relaxed lethargy would be gone in a flash.

The maid removed the scraped-clean plates before setting in front of her a slice of mocha gateau and a silver jug of cream. As Georgia poured herself a liberal helping and picked up her fork to demolish the cake, he remarked, 'So you were hungry, after all.'

'Yes — very.' In spite of her inner apprehensions, she pulled a rueful face.

'Sorry — to be such a pig, I mean.'

'Have you eaten today?'

'Well . . . ' She frowned. It was difficult to remember — almost as if, in that moment when she'd looked up out of her basement window and seen that sleek grey car, the tanned fingers beating that restless tattoo, her whole life had jolted to a halt and then begun all over again, but on a quite different track. And would it ever be the same again?

His eyes were still on her and she went on rather uncertainly, 'I had coffee and a roll before I left Granada this morning. Nothing since then, though — but that's no excuse.'

'For what?'

'For being so greedy.'

'Please.' He raised one lazy hand. 'It gives me pleasure to see you so — enjoy your food.'

'Oh.' There didn't really seem to be anything else to say to such a remark.

'Most women are so obsessed with their figures that they are terrified of over-eating.'

'Well, actually, I'm pretty obsessed with my figure,' she blurted out. 'Not enough of it, I mean.'

'On the contrary, it is quite perfect — lithe and slender as a reed.'

'Oh, please, you don't have to — '

'And whatever you may think of your body, I promise you that very soon I will have taught you to glory in it.' And as she stared at him, her eyes blank with shock, he went on calmly, 'Would you like coffee now?'

'N-no,' she stammered, her mind still reeling from his words.

'Very well.' He got up. 'Let us go, then.'

Georgia slowly got up, her legs so unsteady that she had to press one hand on the table. It was the wrist which had been shackled, and there was a faint ring of bruises.

'Oh, well, back to the dungeons, I suppose.' She tried to speak flippantly, but her voice quivered.

Ramón came across to her, light as a cat on his feet, and stood, thumbs hitched in his belt, his eyes on her. In the candlelight he was even more handsome, the lines of his body even more devastating in those clothes.

'Will you give me your word that if you are allowed back into Isabel's room you will not be foolish?'

His voice was a silk-smooth lure, and the thought of that bed, with its pretty counterpane, was so tempting. And she was so very tired . . .

But then, stiffening her backbone as if with a steel corset, she said, 'Now I'm sure you don't seriously expect me to promise you that.'

'*Dios*!' He gave a harsh laugh. 'No, I don't think that I do.'

He surveyed her for another moment, then said, 'Very well. Come upstairs with me.'

They went past the door to Isabel's suite. So he was going to put her in another room — one without a convenient tree, no doubt. Maybe she'd won this little battle. Maybe — though a glance at his profile as he half turned his head did not reveal a man prostrate from the first ever defeat of his life.

At the far end of the passage he threw open a door. She walked in, then halted abruptly, an arm's length in front of him. This room was very spacious and the bed was a magnificent four-poster, with a carved headboard in dark wood, and rich, indigo-blue silk hangings. The quilted coverlet, also of dark blue silk, was turned down, all ready for someone to slip beneath.

But it was not the bed which brought her up with a sick jolt. It was the sight of a pair of cream jodhpurs slung across a chair, along with a black shirt and a pair of black leather boots.

'Yes, that's right, Georgia.' From behind her the voice purred in her ear. 'You are too much of a responsibility for my staff, and, tempting though it may be, I am not quite prepared to have you sleep in the dungeon — so you are spending the night in this room. My room.' And he added, so that there could be no possibility of her mistaking his meaning, 'With me.'

5

'No!' Georgia, her hands jerking to the neckline of the robe, backed up against the wall. 'No, I won't. I — I'll give you my word that I won't try to escape. I swear it.'

Ramón gave a short laugh, which set her overwrought nerves twanging even more. 'It is too late, *querida.*'

'I'll never get into that bed with you — n-never,' she stammered.

'Oh, but you will. If only because, in the final analysis, I am far bigger and stronger than you are.' As she stared blindly up at him, his lip twisted. 'Why all this maidenly agitation? After all, you have no doubt shared a bed with many men.'

'I . . . ' Her voice froze in her throat.

'Whereas for me it will be in the nature of an experiment. You see, I have never before slept with a woman.'

'You expect me to believe that?' She gave a shrill laugh.

'It is the truth. I am not, of course, *entirely* inexperienced.' He gave a faint smile. 'I have had two lasting relationships, each of which ended by mutual consent, but I did not choose that either woman should share my bed all night. So — ' this time, a crooked little smile ' — you are honoured, *amada mia*.'

'Honoured?' Her voice rose another notch. 'Because I'm the first to be raped in this bed?'

The smile vanished. 'We are already agreed against the need for such crudity. We meet as equals in the game of love, *querida*, so it will be sweet conquest on my part — and equally sweet surrender on yours.'

She bit hard on the inner flesh of her mouth. What could she do? Even if she screamed for help, none of the servants would come — they were far too well-trained. She was alone — and helpless.

'The bathroom is through there. I shall return in half an hour.' And before she could conjure up the feeblest of replies he had gone, and once more she heard the key grate in the lock.

For several minutes she stood, her face blank, her hands twisting over and over in agitation, but at last, drawing a shuddering breath, she went through to the bathroom. It was even more sumptuous than Isabel's, glowing with white and darkly veined marble. A bamboo curtain led to an alcove, and when she switched on the soft wall-lights she saw, among an array of plants — trailing ferns and shiny-leaved monsteras — a huge sunken bath.

She knew that she really ought just to splash her forehead and take a quick shower, but to her weary body that bath was irresistibly inviting. She gazed down into it, then, not giving herself any more time to think, turned on the taps. While the water ran, she opened the bathroom cabinet, found a new toothbrush and cleaned her teeth. Most of the toiletries were masculine — she unscrewed a bottle of aftershave, sniffed and recognised that subtle citrus scent that he carried around with him. But in one corner there was an unopened bottle of carnation bath mousse, so she poured some into the bath, hesitated, then slopped in about half the bottle and slid down through the layer of bubbles.

Lying back with a groan, she closed her eyes. The perfume of carnation was hypnotic, permeating her whole body like a drug, and, half asleep, she felt herself drift into a twilight world of shadows where someone waited for her, arms outstretched. A cruel little smile played round his lips, but, like all cruel smiles, it did not reach anywhere near his eyes.

'Georgia,' he said softly.

'Wh-what do you want?' She heard a voice — her own, tremulous.

'Come to me.'

'No.'

'Oh, *querida*, you have denied

yourself too long. Come here — I am waiting for you. Georgia . . . '

Her eyes flew open and, too shaken for a moment to focus, she finally made out Torres — her dream had become reality — down on his haunches beside the bath.

'Oh!' With a convulsive movement, which sent a tidal wave of carnation foam over the rim of the bath to lap his feet, she ducked under the suds. 'G-get out of here.'

He was leaning over her, those lean, hard thighs just on a level with her eyes . . .

'If you really had not wanted me in here, you should have locked the door.' Georgia suppressed a groan of anguish. How could she have been so stupid? 'But it is as well that you did forget — it is dangerous to sleep in the bath. Get out, now.'

He raised his hands as though to lift her out but she shied away.

'No, I can manage.'

'Very well.'

He dropped a white bath-towel just by the gold taps, then rose and disappeared through the bamboo curtain. She waited until the door closed, then, very wide awake now, hauled herself out and picked up the towel.

When she emerged, the robe tightly belted around her slim waist, he was lounging in an armchair, one leg crossed over the other. He had taken off his tie — it lay coiled on the dressing-table — and undone the top button of his shirt, revealing the strong column of his throat and, in the V of his white shirt, a sprinkle of fine dark hairs.

As she hesitated, one hand on the tie of the robe, the other still clutching the doorknob, he stood up.

'I shall not be long.'

'Oh, please.' Tension sharpened her voice. 'Take all night.'

He stood looking down at her as she faced him, her back against the door-jamb, her head defiantly set. Then, very slowly, he lifted one hand and, taking a damp curl which lay over her brow, twined his finger in it. He tugged it, just hard enough to make her wince inwardly, then repeated softly, 'I shall not be long.'

The door closed behind him and she leaned up against it, expelling the anger and the fear in one long, juddering breath. As she straightened up she saw, lying on the silk coverlet, her white broderie anglaise nightie. She went over to it and picked it up, holding it to her, her eyes dark and abstracted as they rested on the two pillows.

If she resisted him, would he grow tired of the sport of seduction and, despite his assurance, resort to cruder methods, crushing her protests in his strong arms?

From behind the closed door came the sound of the shower. In her mind's eye Georgia saw the water cascading over that sleek, powerful body and, way beneath the anger and the fear, other sensations stirred in her. Could she resist him? The feelings he roused in her were totally unlike those she had felt for any other man. Basic, over-whelming sexual desire was something she had never thought to experience herself — she had schooled herself resolutely against it — but she could guess just how easy it would be to yield to it. Yield — and then know a lifetime of regret.

The shower was switched off abruptly and, rousing herself, Georgia tore off the robe and pulled on the nightdress, tying the ribbons at the neckline. Turning down one side of the bed, she saw that the sheets were silk, the palest eau-de-Nil. She rested her hand on one, softly stroking the cool, sensuous fabric, then, scuttling over to the window, she opened the shutters sufficiently to let in a thread of moonlight, switched off the lights and slid down between the silken sheets.

The door opened, and for an instant Ramón, a towel slung casually round his hips, was silhouetted, a dark outline in the glow of light from the bathroom. She closed her eyes tightly, ears strained for every sound, hearing him pull the light cord, drop his clothes on a chair, then finally pad across to the bed. It dipped slightly on her side as he sat down on it.

'Georgia.'

For a second she thought of feigning sleep, but then murmured reluctantly, 'Yes?'

'I should perhaps warn you — ' his voice was a languid caress in the warm darkness ' — that since the age of five I have slept naked — and I see no reason tonight to change the habit of thirty years.'

'Well, no, of course you wouldn't,' she muttered, trying desperately to obliterate the insidious image of that superb body — naked.

'Oh, and just one other thing, *querida* . . . ' His voice mocked her. 'In case you are wondering, you are quite safe tonight.' Her eyes jerked open, and he laughed softly. 'This has been quite a day for you. When we make love, I do not intend that fatigue will dull your responses to me. So those mutual delights are postponed — for a short while.'

Raising his fingers to his lips, he kissed the tips softly then brushed the same fingertips across her mouth. 'Goodnight, little spitfire.'

As she lay rigid, he got up then slid into the other side of the bed and seemed to drift immediately into easy sleep.

Georgia, though, lay on the very edge of her portion of the bed, staring into the darkness. Her mouth felt warm, the skin prickling as though with heat rash from where that finger-kiss had brushed her lips. Fiercely, she rubbed them to erase it, but it was no use — her mouth was still tingling, just as though it was asking for more.

So he'd chosen to spare her tonight. But that only left tomorrow, and the next day and the next . . . and the nights . . . Despairingly, she turned on her side, away from him. She wouldn't sleep, of course, not a wink all night — maybe she'd just close her eyes . . .

★ ★ ★

The crack of moonlight had changed to dazzling sunshine. Georgia, surfacing from a deep ocean of sleep, yawned, stretched, then became very still. Maybe it was all a horrible dream. But the sheet she lay on was eau-de-Nil silk, and now, when with extreme reluctance she slowly turned her gaze, there was a dark head on the next pillow. Ramón, though, was still fast asleep.

Her mouth twisted. For the first time in her life — whatever he might choose to believe — she had woken beside a man. Strange, really, how their parents' unhappy example had affected her and Grant so similarly, and yet so differently. Her brother, seemingly unable to form deep relationships, went from one shallow, short-lived attachment to another, while she had erected a barrier against all attachments, shallow or otherwise.

Drawn by — what? — curiosity, or some other feeling she could not analyse, she lay on her side studying Ramón. In sleep it was a softer face, as if its owner had temporarily dropped his guard. The mouth seemed almost to smile, the harsh lines had disappeared, the imperious frown was masked by the untidy black lock of hair that flopped across the brow. That gleam in his eyes was hidden by black lashes, so thick that they shadowed the cheekbones. Pity about those two scratches, she thought wryly — but they would soon fade, and they didn't spoil his looks, not in the least.

And then, without any warning, the lashes fluttered and he was looking straight at her. '*Buenos dias*, Georgia.'

Crimson-faced at being caught out, she turned her head sharply away and did not speak.

'I trust you slept well?'

His lazy drawl infuriated her. 'No thanks to you if I did,' she snapped, eyes on the blue hangings above her.

'Oh, please.' He sounded pained. 'Let us put all the unpleasantnesses of yesterday behind us. Another lovely summer morning, and I open my eyes to see a beautiful woman in my bed.'

'Beautiful!' The brittle laugh came out before she could prevent it.

'Yes, beautiful. Why do you laugh?'

'Don't,' she said, suddenly unsure. 'Don't joke with me, please. Of course I'm not.'

'Georgia.' Before she could move, he had propped himself on one elbow, and with his free hand turned her face round to meet his gaze. The remnants of that little sleeping smile still hovered round his lips. 'You are beautiful.'

'I told you — ' she began angrily, but he overrode her.

'Creamy skin, smooth as this silken sheet, awaiting the touch of a lover's hands . . . ' For an instant, she saw in her mind his hands roving over her flesh. 'Eyes that mirror every thought, that flash fire — or melt into tenderness. That generous, giving mouth . . . '

'No, please . . . ' she tried to say, but his thumb, softly covering her lips, thickened her voice until it died.

'And that wonderful hair — you look like a pale, slender flame, braving the wind.'

'Slender? Skinny, more like,' she said tightly.

'Slender,' he repeated unhurriedly, 'and perfect. And very soon — ' his voice dropped to a husky murmur ' — I shall convince you of that perfection. But in the meantime it is incredible that an experienced woman of — what is it? — twenty-five should still exude such an aura of complete innocence. It is an art which very few women have acquired.'

An art? That was how he was determined to see her. As the stiletto of pain stabbed viciously through her, she retorted, 'And you've obviously acquired the seducer's art, complete with silver tongue — but don't waste your time on me.'

He laughed softly. 'Quite right, *querida*. There is no need for seduction — but — ' rolling away from her, he picked up his watch from the bedside table ' — time is, regrettably, against us this morning. I shall use the bathroom first, as I have various orders to give before we leave.'

'Leave?' She swallowed. 'Wh-where are you taking me?'

He gave her a lazy smile. 'Oh, I thought you might enjoy a few days by the sea.'

'By the . . . You mean Marbella? But I've told you, there's no point. Grant isn't — '

'No, not Marbella,' he said smoothly.

'So you're trying further along the coast for Isabel?' Her heart leapt. Did he, after a night's sleep, believe her, after all? 'Yes, she might — '

'I have given instructions for the search to be intensified in the Marbella area,' he cut in, 'but I have no doubt that she is at this moment either — how did you put it? — somewhere in the Mediterranean or halfway to the Azores.'

'With Grant, you mean?' Her heart

plummeted like a stone.

'Of course. And if he is not due back for two weeks or more, well, we shall just have to resign ourselves to waiting.'

'Look, Ramón . . . ' Oh, what was the use? Anger and frustration raged in her.

'First of all, though, I have an appointment at eleven this morning, so . . . '

Reaching for the towel, which he had carelessly flung down across the bed the night before, he pulled back the sheet and, as she quickly averted her eyes, knotted the towel round him. Sliding open the wardrobe door, he took out an armful of clothes then disappeared into the bathroom and Georgia could do nothing but lie back and listen to the shower, her fingers pleating and unpleating the silk sheet.

When he emerged, he was wearing a pair of casual cream cotton trousers and a chocolate-brown polo shirt which left his tanned arms bare. He came across to the bed and she could smell the faint tang of citrus.

'Get up now.' When she kept her mouth tightly shut and stared at the opposite wall, he added, his voice hardening a fraction, 'I do not wish you to keep me waiting. Do you hear me?' Leaning forward, he rested his fists on the bed, imprisoning her between them.

'Yes, I hear you,' she snarled. 'And no, I won't keep you waiting, damn you.'

'Good. I am glad you understand the situation.'

For a long moment their eyes held, and once again those intangible threads seemed to stir in the still air and twine themselves between them. Finally, though, he smiled — a brief, satisfied smile — straightened, and went out.

How could it happen like this? Georgia asked herself despairingly. She hated him, he despised her, and yet, out of this mutual anatagonism came mutual attraction. People said, didn't they, that love and hate were opposite sides of a narrow coin? This man was her enemy. That she could ever feel anything remotely like love for him was quite impossible, but she was beginning fearfully to wonder whether the other side of hate could really be desire, passion, lust — call it what you wanted. Very soberly, she went through to the bathroom, and found it filled with the scent of him . . .

When she arrived in the hall, María was hovering, to take her to the breakfast-room, smaller than the other imposing room but filled with sunlight. Ramón was already seated at the table, a cup of coffee in one hand, a sheaf of papers in the other. He glanced up casually; she saw his eyes narrow, then he put down his cup.

'Come over here.'

She went, wishing desperately, now it was too late, that she had obeyed her instinct for self-preservation, and stood in front of him.

He gazed at the large green frog in the middle of the loose white T-shirt and read aloud, "Kiss me, I may be a

117

prince.'' His patrician nostrils seemed to dilate, as if they had an unpleasant smell of drains under them.

'It's even better on the back,' she said pertly.

'Turn round.'

When she did so, he silently took in the smug-looking frog and the bold caption, 'That fooled you'.

'*Dios.*' He looked quite ill, she thought, with mingled satisfaction and trepidation. 'Why did you not wear something of Isabel's?' he enquired icily.

'Because they don't fit me. I'm skinny — remember?' She jutted her chin haughtily.

'Or something — different — of your own?'

'I like this T-shirt,' she said defiantly. 'One of Grant's girlfriends gave it to him. It's not his style, though — and it *is* mine. And I'm not changing.' Thrusting her hands into her jeans pockets, she shot him a glowering look. 'I'm on holiday — in case you've forgotten — and I wear things like this on holiday.'

He sighed heavily. 'I had hoped that you'd learned a lesson over your childish attempts to provoke me.'

So had Georgia, actually. With the memories of yesterday still a fresh wound in her mind, she had made a resolution not to spar with him on every occasion. But somehow that T-shirt had been a statement which, not of her own volition, she'd been forced to make.

'Coffee?'

He picked up a ceramic pot and glanced at her, brows raised. She stared down at him, nonplussed. What was going on? Wasn't he going to demand that she change — or tear the shirt off her back?

'Er — yes, please,' she murmured, and slid into her place, just managing to keep a smile of elation off her face. She'd won — she'd actually won a battle with him. And if she'd won a battle, perhaps she could win the war.

* ★ * ★ * ★ *

As Ramón manoeuvred out of the stable block, Georgia sank back into the superb upholstery, trying to look as though she had ridden around in sleek grey Ferraris every day of her life. They drove down through lovely wooded grounds where, in a ring-fence paddock, they passed half a dozen horses — even to Georgia's unpractised eye, pedigree to their last drop of blue blood.

'Those are my polo ponies.'

'They're *beautiful*.'

She watched two pale grey ones, arching proud necks and skittering round one another like ballet dancers. He pulled over and extracted a bag from under the dashboard.

'Come and meet them.'

The horses came prancing up, one a cream mare, and when Ramón stroked her nose she whinnied softly, nuzzling at him. He spoke to her in Spanish, tender little endearments, as he gave

120

her a lump of sugar.

'This is Leila.'

'The one whose fetlock-cream you used on me last night?' she asked with a sideways look.

'That's right,' he replied blandly. 'How is your neck, by the way?'

'Oh, fine, thanks.'

'Let me see.' He tilted her head towards him and ran his fingers along the line of her neck, softly probing. He was very near to her — she was aware of his nearness in every pore of her body, and surely he must hear her sudden unsteady breathing. 'I am sorry. Does that hurt?'

Their eyes met and held for a long moment before hers flickered away.

'N-no, not at all. It — it really must be a miracle cream.' She took a step away from him. 'What a lovely horse. May I give her some sugar?'

'No — better not. She is very jealous of other women.'

'Jealous? But she's a horse.'

He grinned, showing strong white

teeth. 'Don't let her hear you say that — she thinks she is my favourite mistress.'

'Oh.' Georgia looked up at him uncertainly.

'You can give some to the others, though.' He handed her the bag. 'This young one here is Leila's colt. Put it on the flat of your hand — like this.'

Holding her wrist, he tipped out some lumps. A small though aristocratic nose came through the rails, and a pair of velvet lips gently took the sugarlumps.

'Oh, he's lovely.' She stroked the silky nose, laughing aloud with pleasure.

When she looked round at Ramón, though, she saw that he was watching her, and at the expression in his eyes her pulses leapt and she swung away . . .

Back on the drive, bordered by the tall cypresses now, Georgia cleared her throat, breaking a silence which had lasted several minutes. 'Where do you play polo?'

'Oh, near Madrid. And in South America — Argentina, especially.'

'Have you ever played in England?'

'Quite often at Cowdray — and Windsor, of course.'

'Windsor?' Her eyes were like amber saucers. 'You mean . . . ?'

'Naturally,' he replied gravely. 'You surely know me well enough by now, *querida*, to be sure that I only take on the best.' And, changing down as they approached the wrought-iron gates, he turned out on to the road and accelerated away.

Georgia watched the countryside, browned by the heat of summer, slip past her window, and felt strangely disembodied. This time yesterday she had been bowling along a similar road, bordered by plane trees, a village ahead, the jagged black mountains, which you never seemed to be very far from in Spain, a backdrop to the white walls and red roofs. She'd been a totally free agent — just the way she liked it — exulting in the feel of the machine beneath her eating up the open road.

Since then, all control of her life had been wrested away from her, and the strange thing was that, while that thought was unnerving — no, frightening — it somehow gave today a dream-like quality.

Ahead now was the Mediterranean, dark blue under a heat haze. Ramón followed the coast road for a few miles, then abruptly swung the car down a narrow, dusty track which bumped along for a couple of hundred yards then opened out to a stunning view.

They were above a narrow valley, almost a cleft, which dropped to a tiny beach and the sea. A stream meandered down in a series of muddy pools, all but dried up at this time of year, and trickled over the beach to meet the sea. The scene was far from peaceful, though. Building work was in full swing; workmen swarmed all over the site and the air echoed to the sound of concrete-mixers and drills.

'Well, what do you think of my baby?'

Ramón leaned forward, resting his elbows on the steering-wheel.

'This is yours?'

'Yes, every centimetre. This was the final toe-hold in Spain that my ancestor held on to before he was able to go back inland, and it has been in our family ever since. I built that house — ' she followed his pointing finger and saw, half hidden among the trees on the opposite side of the valley, a low white villa ' — but I'm so busy and get down here so seldom that I decided to put the land to better account.'

'Developing it, you mean?' She pulled a face. 'But if you're not careful, that could ruin it. I — I mean — ' She broke off in confusion, but he laughed.

'It could do, yes, if it were not handled sympathetically. But I intend to learn from others' mistakes, so don't worry,' he went on. 'Everything at La Herradura will be the height of — how would you put it? — good taste. And after all, why should I not share all this beauty — ' his sweeping gesture took in the entire valley, and a fair proportion of the land behind it ' — with others who can also appreciate it?'

'And who can also afford to pay for it,' she put in slyly.

He gave her a level look. 'But of course. My estates do not run themselves — these days, they must earn their keep. I shall show you round later, but first — ' he glanced at his watch ' — I have that meeting, so I must leave you. Come up to the villa — you can amuse yourself in the swimming-pool.'

'No, thank you.' She bridled at his patronising tone. 'I'll *amuse* myself far more down here.'

He looked faintly surprised, then shrugged. 'As you wish. If you are bored, you can always go down on to the beach.'

'I shan't be bored — not in the least,' she replied blandly, opening the door. She reached for her shoulder-bag, but he caught hold of the strap.

'I think I'll keep this for you.' When she glared at him he added, very pleasantly, 'Please — do not try anything that you might regret. As you will observe, there is a security fence — complete with guards — primarily, of course, to keep undesirables *out*, but its role can very easily be reversed. So — ' as she slammed the door and turned away ' — take care.' And, with a wave, he was gone.

Georgia made her way carefully down through the site, meeting curious glances and the odd wolf-whistle, Spanish variety, before halting at the level ground between the development and the beach. What a perfect setting it was. Up there was the villa, surrounded by cypress trees, arching bamboos and hibiscus. It must have been paradise before the workmen moved in — just a hidden green valley and a small silver-sand beach. What had Ramón said? 'I'm so busy ... ' For some reason, that thought saddened her, and to shake herself clear of it she went across and sat under a palm-tree.

What a wonderful opportunity for a

landscape designer. She felt a twinge of envy for whoever Ramón had chosen to draw up the plans. What would they have chosen to do? The valley, narrow, almost claustrophobic, was crying out for the Moorish style — and that would surely appeal to him, with his haughty pride in his ancestry. Tiers of white apartments were already rising, one on the other, on both sides. That stream, though — what would she do . . . ?

Pencil — paper. Fingers twitching, she reached for her bag, then remembered and leaned back against the rough bark, gnawing her lip in frustration. But then, on an impulse, she knelt down and carefully smoothed out the sandy ground in front of her. Taking up a stick, she began sketching . . .

* * *

'Playing at sandcastles?'

The caustic voice penetrated the very edge of her consciousness but then a pair of feet appeared, one shoe brushing her fingertips.

'No, don't,' she said sharply as the foot went to scuff through the mounded sand.

She sat back abruptly on her heels, pushing the curls off her damp forehead and flexing her aching spine. She had been totally absorbed for what could have been hours, but now she looked up at him and, shading her eyes against the sun, saw with a sickening lurch of her stomach that Ramón was scowling furiously down at her.

6

'Wh-what's wrong? I haven't done anything,' Georgia said defensively.

'No. Just for once, you haven't.' The scowl deepened and he kicked out at a harmless piece of driftwood, sending it flying.

'What's wrong, Ramón?' she heard herself repeating.

He hunched a morose shoulder. 'Oh, problems.'

'Do you want to tell me about them?' she asked hesitantly. 'It helps to talk sometimes. Grant always — '

'I'm sure he does,' he snarled. 'But not in this case — it's merely a question of my misjudgement.' Raking his fingers through his hair, he let out a long, angry breath. 'What have you been doing with yourself? And what is this?'

'Oh, nothing,' she said hastily, throwing away her stick. 'Just doing as you told me — amusing myself.'

She got up, grimacing as pins and needles prickled through her feet, then went to obliterate the pattern in the sand with her toe, but he caught hold of her by the arm.

'No, don't do that. What is it?'

'Well — ' she laughed a little shamefacedly ' — actually I've been doing a three-dimensional design for La Herradura — why do you call it that, by the way?'

'From the shape. It means horse-shoe,' he replied, his eyes still on the complicated pattern in the sand. 'Show me.'

'Oh, no. I — '

'Show me.' Going down on his haunches, he pointed an imperious finger, and reluctantly she came down beside him.

'Well, those are the two sides of the valley, and this is the linking tier at the back. I've put narrow walkways around them, and high inner walls. There'd be lots of plants — bougainvillaea, that

131

sort of thing — tumbling over them, so there'd be a series of small, shaded courtyards, to give it a Moorish feel, you see.'

She looked up into the narrow face beside her, but it was expressionless, so she went on, 'And you must — I mean, *I* would use the water. I'd have a storage cistern, and a pump, of course, built in under the lip of the hill up there — ' she gestured above them, but his eyes did not leave the design ' — and I'd bring it down the hillside in little rocky pools and streams.'

'And what about that?' A lean finger jabbed at the centre of the model.

'Oh, that's the plaza — Moorish again. But of course you know that.' She gave him a sidelong glance. 'A pool, maybe in a tiled alcove — those lovely blue-green tiles they use so much — a fountain, a cobbled courtyard, and little mysterious alleys leading off among the trees and shrubs.'

'And that?' Another jab.

'Oh, that's where we are now

— there'd be a bigger pool, like an oasis. We'd keep — '

'We?' He raised an enquiring brow.

'No, I mean — ' colouring, she hastily corrected herself ' — I'd keep these palm-trees, of course, and put in some clumps of bamboo. And those apartments over there — ' this time he did glance up, towards the half-finished structures ' — I'd put their balconies on stilts and run the pool underneath them . . . '

His gaze had shifted back to her, and her voice died away. 'Well, that's what I'd do.' She smiled a shade self-consciously and, brushing the sand off her jeans, scrambled to her feet.

'What is your job, Georgia?'

She could not resist an impish smile. 'I'm a landscape architect, of course.'

'I see. So you don't just do — this and that.'

He leaned back against the tree, regarding her thoughtfully, and, edgy under his scrutiny, she retorted, 'Don't tell me — you're one of those chauvinists who disapprove of women having careers. I suppose you think that a woman's place is in the kitchen, the bedroom and the nursery.'

'No,' he replied unsmilingly. 'In my case, I do not think that.'

'Oh.' She stared at him, disconcerted, then recovered herself. 'You astonish me, *Señor.*'

'You see, *Señorita* — ' his voice lightly mocked her ' — in my position I can afford to employ staff in the kitchen and nursery, which only leaves the — '

'I know what that leaves,' she snapped, cursing inwardly for having got herself into this particular little tussle.

'What was your training?' he asked abruptly.

'I have a diploma from the Institute of Design in London.'

'And what commissions have you received?'

'Well — not much for the first year.' She smiled. 'I mainly persuaded family and friends to let me redesign their gardens and patios.'

'You mean, you talked them into submission?' His voice was ironic.

She gave him a cool look. 'Maybe — but they were all pleased with the results. Anyway, since then I've expanded. I did the landscaping for a big out-of-town shopping complex — that was as part of a team, of course.'

'You're telling me that you were able to work with other people? Astonishing.'

'And — ' she refused to be baited ' — I've just finished designing the grounds for the latest Brennan hotel.'

'Brennan! And do they approve?'

'I think so,' She pulled a wry face. 'From what I saw of Tyler Brennan, he'd have let me know soon enough if my work wasn't up to standard.'

'Yes, I imagine he would,' he said drily, then all at once straightened up. 'Right, let's go.'

'Where to?' she demanded, suspicion flaring in her.

He turned back to her, that slight

frown settling on his black brows again. 'Up to the villa, of course, for lunch. Where else?'

'No, I'd rather stay here.' Here in the open, under the gaze of the workmen taking their siesta sprawled beneath the shade of those trees up there. Here, where I'm safe from —

'You are impossible,' he remarked, cutting into her thoughts. Without warning, his still simmering fury was turned on her. 'Always difficult — '

'*Me*?'

'Always no, no, no.'

'I'm only — '

'Why not, just for once, smile and say, But of course, Ramón — and stop fighting me?'

Because if I once stop fighting you I'm going to fall — very heavily — for you, and that's something I don't intend to do with any man. The words bubbled up into Georgia's mind like ice-cold spring water, so shocking that, bereft of speech, she could only stare up at him.

'Well?' he snarled. 'No answer?'

'I . . . ' She gulped, then said unsteadily, 'No, no answer.'

'Oh, *querida*.' Just as quickly, the angry tiger's snarl was gone and he went on, as though to himself, 'What she does to me, this Georgia Leigh. It is incredible. We are all identical — all of us formed from water, blood, bone, sinew — and yet never has there been in the history of this planet another Georgia Leigh. I swear it.'

'Of course not.' She tossed back her copper curls. 'I'm unique.'

'I should hope you are,' he said grimly. 'And I wonder if the world knows what a lot it has to be grateful for.'

Lifting his hand, he very gently stroked her face, running his fingers across her lips, over her cheekbones, the tip of her straight little nose, just as if he was exploring it, as if he had never touched a face before, and she could only stand, her lips parted, staring back at him. He was frowning very slightly to himself, then, when he met her gaze, his fingers stilled, and their eyes held for half a dozen of her fluttering heartbeats. But then, very slowly, he let his hand drop and, turning, strode off up the narrow track.

Ramón was waiting for her on the wide terrace of the villa, seated in a padded chair, tapping his fingers impatiently on the arm, when she came toiling up the steep driveway between the massed trees and shrubs.

'Are we having lunch out here? That will be — '

'Lunch? Oh, later,' he said dismissively. 'Come with me.'

He led the way indoors, through a large sitting-room and into another room whose shutters were tightly closed. He flung them back, exposing wide picture windows giving a panoramic view of the sea and, immediately beneath them, a bird's-eye view of the tiers of half-finished apartments.

'This is my office when I am here.'

'It has a lovely view, but . . . '

Why on earth have you brought me here? she was going to say, but Ramón was already dragging a mahogany desk across to the window. He followed it with a huge swivel chair, the twin of the one in his office back in the castle. From a filing cabinet he fetched a stack of paper, then set down pens and pencils on the desk.

'Sit down.'

'But — '

Seizing her by the elbows, he propelled her towards the chair and pushed her down into it.

'I want you to prepare landscape designs for the development. You will have to take account of the building progress to date, but that will be no problem,' he added calmly. 'You have already plotted it out down on the beach.'

'But . . . ' she said again. Coherent speech seemed to be impossible — something had happened to her vocal cords. She cleared her throat. 'I don't understand. Surely you've already hired a landscape designer, at the same time as you chose the architect?'

'Yes, I did,' he replied grimly. 'Two actually. I fired the first three months ago — ' he paused, and somehow Georgia knew what was coming ' — and the second this morning.'

'But why?' Her heart was beginning to beat faster. 'I mean — surely you wouldn't have given the commission to anyone incompetent in the first place?'

'They were not incompetent — they just failed to see things my way. Both of them came up with bland, non-assertive designs — technically correct, no doubt, but which could have been placed anywhere in the world. Those were the latest effort.' He gestured towards a pile of paper in the waste-bin. 'I tore them up in front of him.'

'I see.' A tremor of sympathy for her unfortunate fellow designer ran through her.

'So I want *you* to produce a design for me — now.'

'But that's impossible.' Georgia stared

at him, horrified. 'I take weeks — months sometimes — over a project. I can't hurry them.'

'Nonsense. You were doing well enough down there.'

'Yes, but — '

'But what?' he demanded

'If you must know, it's one thing to play games in the sand — it's quite another to put a design down on paper for your hypercritical eye.'

'I am not hypercritical. I merely know what I want, and am impatient when others cannot see it.'

'You can say that again,' she muttered. She couldn't do it — wouldn't — and, as she remembered his expression when he had arrived on the beach, her insides lurched in apprehension. 'No, it's out of the question. I — I'm not experienced enough.'

He gave her a slanting cat's smile across the desk. 'Is the *unique* Georgia Leigh telling me she is backing away from a challenge? That she is a coward?'

Unable to meet his eyes, she flicked a

141

thumb-nail along the leather tooling on the desk edge.

'*Querida.*' His voice dropped to a seductive purr. 'I know you are afraid of me — ' she tensed, but still did not look at him ' — but regard me merely as any other potential client.'

'Yes, just a hundred more times more difficult than any others I've come up against,' she muttered sullenly.

He was right, though, damn him. She *was* afraid of him — afraid of the effect he had on her leaping pulses, afraid of the hunger she felt stir in her when she saw that lean, hard body, at it was now, propped against the desk, the long legs stretched in front of it. But she had to fight him, and keep on fighting.

'I'm not afraid of you,' she said stoutly, and saw him raise a mocking brow half a millimetre. 'I just don't want to be thrown into the dungeons if you don't happen to like my designs.'

'Oh, there are many other ways of showing my disapproval, I assure you,' he replied silkily. 'You know your problem, Georgia? You simply cannot accept the fact that someone has a stronger will than yours. You *will* bend to me. I mean to teach you to do that, and it would be so much simpler if you accept that — now.'

Before she could reply, Ramón pushed himself up from the desk. 'You will stay here until you produce at least some preliminary drafts for me. And to make sure — ' by this time he was over by the door, withdrawing the key from the lock ' — I shall lock you in.'

'Not again!' She half got to her feet, then sank down again.

'And there is no way out — not even for you.'

'You can't *do* this to me,' she wailed.

He leaned an elbow on the doorjamb. 'But as you see, I can. When you have finished, knock on the door and you will be released.'

'And what about my lunch?' she hurled after him, but the door had already closed.

She snapped her heels down on the

marble tiles, sending the chair spinning round and round. At last it came to a halt and, chin cupped on her fist, she sat staring out across the sea, her eyes as stormy as the Mediterranean was blue and placid. What a nerve, what an absolute nerve that man had. No wonder that ward of his had taken off. If the girl had any sense, she'd still be travelling — fast.

Georgia frowned down at the array of pens and pencils. Had he ever been married? Surely no woman would ever, even for the life of luxurious ease that Torres could offer, have surrendered her independence to such a chauvinistic swine? And anyway, what had he said last night about never having shared his bed with a woman? Last night . . .

But even as she thrust that image fiercely away the thought came — to win the love of such a man, to be held in his arms, against his heart . . . Wouldn't that make up for being told what to wear, what to do, what not to do . . . what to *think*? No, of course it wouldn't. Oh, some women might consider it worthwhile, but not Georgia Leigh — not in a million years.

She stared at the pile of pristine white paper just in front of her. It was very tempting to sit here, with her feet up on the desk, until he graciously chose to unlock the door. Tempting, but at the thought of his reaction her spirit quailed. And besides — her eyes strayed to the scene below the window — what a challenge it would be, to create beauty out of chaos and mud, and to stun Ramón with her abilities — though she knew him well enough by now to be sure that he wasn't a man to be over-easily impressed. Even so . . . Pulling the top sheet of paper towards her, she took up a pencil . . .

* * *

Behind her, the door opened.

'What?' Irritably, she stopped, her pencil poised over the paper. Then, as a pair of long legs appeared at her elbow,

145

she scowled up at him. 'Go away. I haven't finished.'

'Yes, you have — for today, at least.' And Ramón neatly tweaked the pencil out from between her fingers.

'No. I must finish it.' She snatched up another pencil, but his hand closed over her wrist like a steel trap.

'Drop it.'

'No.' She watched in glowering silence as he peeled back her fingers and removed it, then tossed it back on to the table.

'Why didn't you eat your lunch — weren't you hungry after all?'

'Lunch?' She looked round blankly, then saw that on a corner of the desk someone had placed a tray of cold meat, bread, cheese, salad, a bowl of fruit and a carafe of white wine. Someone had placed it there — and someone else had taken a couple of bites out of the bread, but no more.

When she glanced up enquiringly, he said, 'Rosalia, my housekeeper, told me that you hardly seemed to notice her.'

'Sorry.' She came to at last. Her eyes still glazed, her mind still more than half on the paper in front of her, she realised that at some time the drills had fallen silent and dusk had settled on the valley beneath them. She pulled a rueful face. 'I always lose myself when I'm working.'

'So I observe,' he said drily, 'but for now you have done enough. Show me.'

'No, not till it's — '

'Yes.'

Before she could cover them with her elbows, he slid out the sheaf of papers, glancing at each in turn before dropping it on to the desk. Georgia sat back in the swivel chair, trying to appear nonchalant. If he didn't like them — well, too bad, she told herself fiercely. She didn't care a jot for his opinion. But it was no use — she knew that, more than with any other plans she had ever prepared, she desperately craved his approval.

But when he finished his leisurely perusal of the final diagram, he let it fall back on top of the rest with no comment, his face expressionless. She wanted to bang her fists down on the desk and shout, Well, do you like them, damn you? And if you don't — so what? I *know* that it would be the finest thing I've ever done.

Instead, as she sat forward, looking up at him, she winced suddenly and put her hand to her neck.

'What's the matter?'

'Oh — just a stiff neck. I always get one when I've been working for hours.' Gingerly she moved it, then gave an involuntary little grunt of pain.

'Let me see.' He moved behind the chair.

'No, it'll be all right — I'll just take a couple of pain-killers. That'll stop it — and the lousy headache which usually follows.'

As if to confirm her words, the first stabbing pain began over her right eye, but as she reached for her bag he drew her back into the chair, then, putting his hands flat over her shoulders, began gently massaging the tight muscles. She tensed under his touch but then let go, surrendering to those fingers, which probed the sore spots, easing away the pain. Gradually, he moved up her neck then across her scalp, until, mesmerised by the gentle rhythm, she closed her eyes.

'Is that better?'

Georgia's eyelids fluttered open as he bent round to look into her face, his eyes a hand's length away from hers.

'I . . . ' She half turned her head then cautiously flexed her neck. 'Yes — yes, thank you. That's fine,' she said a little huskily.

'Good.'

He pulled back the chair and before she could move put his hands under her elbows and lifted her out of it. They stood, very close together, his hands still cupped over her elbows, his breath warm on her face. Leaning forward slightly, he brushed his lips across hers, an almost imperceptible caress yet so intensely erotic that it sent tingling

149

currents of electricity radiating out from her mouth to the furthermost nerve-endings of her body.

Her body felt strange, heavy, her bones molten. But then, even as she gave a little sigh against his mouth, he drew back, his eyes narrowed slightly, a faint smile tugging his thin lips. 'Come — I am taking you out to dinner in Nerja.'

'Oh, but I must shower and change,' she protested, adding, in an attempt to regain something of her old familiar vitality, 'You wouldn't want to be seen dead alongside this T-shirt, I'm sure.'

He lifted one shoulder. 'An extreme reaction, perhaps, but no — certainly not tonight.'

She followed him down a passage, that strange heaviness still on her limbs, and he threw open a door. 'This is your suite.'

In the soft glow of wall-lights, Georgia saw a pretty room, furnished in sea-green and white, spiced with touches of jade and navy. Her canvas travel-bag stood on a rush-seat chair, and someone had hung her clothes in the wardrobe.

'You have — ' He glanced at his watch.

'Don't tell me — fifteen minutes,' she said resignedly.

His lips twitched. 'I was about to say twenty, but if you insist — fifteen.'

As soon as he had gone, she went across to the wardrobe. If only she hadn't packed in such a hurry, she thought despairingly. And besides, one small holdall strapped to the bike barely held more than a few T-shirts, shorts, a bikini and toilet things. But she could have brought the new blue silk dress — or the pretty two-piece Grant had bought for her birthday. She scowled at a lime-green cotton skirt. For some reason which she didn't choose to analyse, she wanted to look good tonight — almost as if, having made one statement with the kiss-me frog, she wanted to make quite another this evening.

She half pulled out the skirt, then something else slipped from its hanger. Of course . . . Georgia's heart lifted and she took up the dress, holding it against her. A black slip dress, knee-length, in crinkly polyester which passed — almost — for silk, with a drawstring waist and pencil straps. Quite old, and she'd only brought it because it always crammed into any corner of her bag and came out smiling, but somehow she still looked good in it.

Throwing it down on the bed, she went through to the small tiled shower-room, stripped, and ducked under the shower. Minutes later she finished drying her curls, pulled a wide-tooth comb through them until they turned into a pale copper halo, then studied her face in the wide mirror. Faint traces of her bruise still showed, but somehow she looked different tonight; it was nothing she could put her finger on — but different. Her skin glowed, her eyes, enormous in the light, seemed to have taken on a new softness, while her mouth . . . She stared at her mouth — lips parted, a tremulous smile hovering on them — with a vague feeling of disquiet. It was almost as though she was waiting for something to happen, hovering on the very brink of some momentous event . . .

But of course, that was it. Whenever she was waiting for a prospective client to give her the yea or nay, she was always on a natural high, the adrenalin flowing. Presumably, sooner or later this evening, Ramón would deign to give her his opinion of her plans — so that was all that was wrong with her tonight . . .

She slicked on some coral lip-gloss, a smudge of brown eyeshadow, stared at herself a second longer, then, as though all at once anxious to get away from that other Georgia in the mirror, hurried back into the bedroom, slithered into the dress and snatched up her sandals.

Ramón was waiting for her in the

hall, his back to her, and, barefoot, she did not make a sound. Unseen for a moment, she paused, looking at him, and then he turned. He gazed at her, his eyes, in their own time, taking in every detail from her soft curls, through her body, her slender curves enhanced by the clinging line of the dress, to her naked feet. Something flickered momentarily in his eyes, a muscle tugged at one corner of his mouth, but his voice, when he finally spoke, was fully under control.

'*Buenas tardes*, Georgia. So — your clothes are not limited entirely to motorcycle leathers and green frogs.'

'No, not entirely.' She smiled at him rather uncertainly, then blurted out, before she could hold it back, 'You look very nice.'

He too had changed — into a white denim suit and navy open-necked shirt. The casual lines of the suit flattered his long, lean legs, the colour making him seem darker — more alien, somehow, and she swallowed down a sudden tightness in her throat which was making it almost impossible to catch her breath.

He inclined his head gravely. 'Thank you. Something tells me that it is not easy for a mere male to gain Señorita Georgia Leigh's approbation. Now — sit down.'

He gestured her to a cane chair and, when she sat in it, took her sandals from her. Going down on his haunches in front of her, he slid first one slender foot into its sandal, and then the other. It was a simple, perfectly ordinary action, yet somehow he made the gesture indefinably sexual, so that her skin tingled and her stomach muscles clenched.

Taking her hand, he lifted her to her feet, but then, instead of releasing her hand, carried it to his mouth. He turned it over and, as she stood unprotesting, kissed it, then, parting his lips, ran the tip of his tongue around her palm in little spirals. The friction of his tongue, rigid against her moist skin, all but overwhelmed her in its blatant eroticism.

Finally, though, he raised his eyes to regard her, holding her faltering gaze with a look of infinite promise.

'Time to go,' he murmured softly, and on legs which all but buckled under her she followed him to the car.

7

Ramón parked in one of the side-streets leading into Nerja and they walked into the centre. Georgia was enchanted — narrow winding alleys, tiled housefronts, glimpses between high whitewashed walls into secluded flower-filled courtyards, and sometimes, through white stone archways, the moonlight glinting on basalt-coloured waves.

As they stopped momentarily in one cobbled street to allow a riotous family group to go past, from black-clad great-grandmother to new-born baby snug in his young mother's arms, she stole a glance at Ramón. He looked so right here in this little town which was still so heavily imbued with the alien, non-European air of Moorishness. All he needed were white silk robes and head-dress, that cream mare Leila beneath him, softly jingling her ornate desert harness, and a curved, gold dagger at his belt, to set off to perfection that dark, haughty face, with its hint of lurking cruelty still there, even this evening, when he seemed totally relaxed.

Along with the other pre-dinner strollers they walked out along the palm-fringed Balcon de Europa, the sea shushing softly on either side, the mountains in the distance a dark, jagged silhouette against the blue-black sky. In a window of one of the little shops back in the square was a poster advertising a bullfight in Málaga, and Ramón paused, glancing over it before walking on.

'Do you go — to bullfights, I mean?' Georgia asked, curious about this enigmatic man at her side.

'On occasion. Have you been?'

'Certainly not. It's barbaric.'

He smiled faintly at her vehemence. 'Well, yes, foreigners — especially women — do see it differently from Spaniards.'

'Yes, we do. We see it for what it is — horrible, cruel.'

He looked down at her, the smile still glinting in his grey eyes. 'How fierce you are, *querida* — more than a match for any fighting bull, I'm sure.'

'Don't tease me,' she muttered angrily. 'It's not funny.'

'I agree. The *corrida* is not a joke — it is an ancient art, and the struggle for supremacy between a skilled *torero* and a good bull is a graceful, elegant ballet. Oh, yes,' he insisted as she tried to protest hotly, 'the matador's aim, from his opening passes, is to gain total supremacy over his opponent. However valiant, however stubborn the bull, his will to fight is broken — it *must* be broken — and it is then, and only then, that *el estocada a recibir*, the moment of truth, total, willing submission, is achieved. And that, Georgia — ' as he spoke, his voice had dropped to a low, initimate purr ' — is where the timeless fascination lies. You must surely see that?'

'Well . . . ' Desperately, she tried to regain her former belligerent tone. 'I — '

'Ah, here we are.' And, taking her arm, he steered her beneath a low archway in the white wall into a cobbled courtyard, with a handful of wooden tables and benches lit by candle-lamps . . .

'*Gracias.*' She smiled at the young waiter as he handed them menus and set down a jug of iced water.

'It's a simple place but the food is excellent,' Ramón remarked, 'especially the seafood.'

Opening his menu, he began studying it, but Georgia, under cover of reading hers, covertly watched him, his words about the bullfight still echoing softly in her head. The bull's will to fight is broken — it *must* be broken. Wasn't that how he would see a relationship with a woman; wasn't that what he was trying to do to her — gain total control over her? Those subtle but inescapably erotic gestures earlier this

160

evening — they were the opening passes. How much longer would he delay moving in for the kill — the moment of truth? And when he did, would *her* will be strong enough to deny him his supremacy . . . ?

He glanced up, his eyes meeting hers, holding them as he seemed to reach into her mind, see its turmoil. But all he said, blandly, was, 'Ready to order?'

'Oh, no — not quite.' And she lowered her gaze . . .

The food *was* excellent. Georgia's delicate tuna mousse, served with a fan of sliced avocado, preceded a bouillabaisse served with crusty bread and pats of pale icy cold butter. Ramón had ordered lobster, and between mouthfuls of her own meal she watched him deal with it — as he did everything — swiftly, efficiently, with his long, slightly tapering fingers. How powerful those hands were . . . She knew that, though, didn't she? she thought, with a glance at that faint ring of bruises on her wrist.

Around them the talk and laughter flowed easily to and fro and Georgia, conscious every moment of the tension within her, somehow managed to keep a light, meaningless conversation going. Most of their fellow diners were deeply engrossed in their own affairs, but ever since they'd arrived a couple of elegant, beautifully dressed young women among a group at the next table had been alternately avidly eyeing Ramón and scrutinising her, as though in blank astonishment, she thought with wry amusement.

As she fielded yet another sideways glance of what must surely have been the 'What on earth does a superb masculine specimen like that see in her?' variety, Ramón lifted the bottle of wine from its nest of ice. When he went to fill up her glass, she covered it hastily with her hand.

'Oh, no — I've drunk enough, thanks.'

The white *Rioja*, though light and filled with the scent of summer flowers and fruit, was very strong, and she could feel her head spinning.

'Very well, but we must drink a toast. To your success.'

'As what?'

His mouth tugged in a faint smile. 'Oh, *querida*, what a suspicious mind there is beneath those *encantadores* copper curls. As my landscape designer, of course.'

'Your . . . ' She gaped at him. 'You mean,' she managed at last, 'you liked my drawings?'

'But of course. Didn't I say so?'

'No, you didn't, actually,' she replied tartly.

He spread his hands. 'An oversight. I was extremely impressed. So, that is all settled — while we await your brother's arrival, you will prepare detailed plans for me.'

'Now wait a minute.' Georgia felt breathless, as if she had been caught up by a tidal wave. 'I was just doing those plans — well, for my own amusement. I'm glad you like them, but I'm not at all sure — '

'And if I approve the finished designs — '

'But you don't even know my fees.' Struggling to keep her footing under the tidal wave, she tried to assume her most businesslike manner.

'They are very high, I hope.' When she stared at him, nonplussed, he went on, 'A woman like you, Georgia — ' that intimate purr had slid into his voice again ' — should never sell herself cheaply.'

Across the narrow table his eyes held hers once more, daring them to break free. Seconds passed, the sounds around them falling away to a distant murmur, way beyond the blood pumping in her ears, then he gestured to her glass.

'So, let us drink our toast. What was it again?'

'To my success — that was it, wasn't it? Or maybe it should be to my submission,' she added tightly, her gaze on the stem of the glass as she slowly twirled it between her fingers.

He laughed softly. 'You mean like the two contestants in the arena? Perhaps — although, *amada mia*, the choice, ultimately, is yours.'

'Is it?' she blurted out, too late to bite back the unwise words.

'You know it is, *querida*.' He was so — so damnably sure of himself, she thought despairingly, but this time she crushed any response. 'So — ' he raised his glass ' — to La Herradura.'

'To La Herradura,' she replied mechanically.

'You will, of course, complete the designs within two weeks.'

'But — '

'I shall be busy setting up the next stage of the development — an equestrian centre and eighteen-hole golf course.'

She stared at him, open-mouthed. 'You're not expecting me to design that for you as well, I hope?'

'Of course not,' he replied suavely. 'Golf courses require a highly special-ised expertise — and in any case your days will be fully occupied without that.' He paused, then added very softly, 'The nights, of course, will be a different matter.'

Forcing herself to ignore the challenge in his voice, she said coldly, 'And you expect me to do this in two weeks? I've already told you, a major project like this could take months.'

'In this case, however, two weeks is all you have. Your brother may well have walked into my little snare by then.'

But I don't want him to come! Appalled, she tried desperately to snatch up the image of Grant, stumbling all unknowing into the clutches of this ruthless man. But no — that wasn't the reason why, all at once, she so urgently wanted her twin to stay safe in Marbella. Ramón would surely accept in the end that he had been wrong about him and Isabel. And then what? His bait would be of no further use to him — he would set her free.

But did she want that? To ride off

with Grant, return to the security of England — and never see Ramón again? Yes, of course she did — and yet . . . She had been held prisoner — for that was what it was, however much he might dress it up with civilised evening excursions and fancy job offers — for not much more than a day, but already something inside her was whispering that when the cage door swung open she would cling to the bars, begging not to have to leave.

That was a well-known psychological syndrome, though, wasn't it, the prisoner shying away from his longed-for liberty? And there was that other one of the female hostage conceiving an overwhelming, wholly irrational sexual passion for her captor. Was that what was happening to her? Raw panic gripped her, and her hand shook so violently that some of her wine spilled on to the table.

But at least she was fully aware of what could happen. She knew the dangers, so surely she could keep them

— and Ramón — at bay . . . ?

'I — ' She had to break off to swallow down the tightness in her throat, and he raised his dark brows enquiringly. 'If I do take on this assignment — and I haven't agreed to that yet — I shall need proper working materials.'

'Such as?'

'Drawing-boards, some decent paper, draught-compasses — all the things I have back in my studio in London.'

He shrugged. 'That's no problem. We can set you up now, this evening — and that might even help you to make up your mind.' As if she really had any choice, Georgia thought bitterly they both knew that. 'But first, coffee?'

'No, thank you.'

'*Bueno.*' And, catching the hovering waiter's eye, he drew out his wallet.

Outside, the streets were still thronged with strollers — locals and tourists, all enjoying the balmy late summer night as Ramón guided her down a narrow alley and into a shop selling artists' materials. Leaning back against the counter, he watched as she assembled the goods she needed, only moving forward to peel more notes from his wallet and give crisp directions for the dispatch of the bulky parcel the following morning.

Out in the square again, instead of turning towards the street where the car was parked, he turned down yet another lane which led to a small plaza near the church where there were several boutiques. One was a dress-shop — horrendously expensive, to judge from the couple of designer-label dresses draped ultra-casually in the window. On the doorstep, Georgia stopped dead.

'What are we going in here for?' Her voice bristled with suspicion.

'While you are working for me, you will be dressed appropriately.'

'No more green frogs, you mean?'

'Precisely.'

'No, wait.'

She put a hand on his arm, but then withdrew it swiftly. There was so much physical energy in the man that, as she'd touched him, it was as if an electric current had run through her palm and into her body.

'Look,' she went on in an urgent whisper, 'there's one thing I must make clear.'

'Yes?' He moved gracefully aside to allow a couple of elderly but extremely chic women past.

'Setting me up in working materials is one thing, but this — ' she gestured towards the interior of the shop ' — is altogether different. You may be buying my professional services, but you aren't buying me.'

'But of course not, *querida*. I would not dream of such an insult as offering to buy you.' Georgia just had time to relax a fraction. 'No such sordidly mercenary considerations will ever be necessary for us to make love.'

And his hand was over her elbow, steering her inexorably into the elegant little shop . . .

★   ★   ★

'Try this now. It will suit you, I am sure.' He thrust yet another dress at her, a sliver of pale maize-gold silk.

'No — no more, *please*, Ramón,' she begged in an undertone, conscious not only of the pile of clothes on the ornate table — nothing so plebeian as a counter here — but of the close attention of the smartly dressed young woman who appeared to be the manageress. For the last hour she'd been paraded up and down the velvety pink carpet, exactly as though she were a thoroughbred mare in the sale-ring and he a highly discriminating prospective buyer, and her nerves were becoming increasingly frayed.

'Just this one.'

'Oh, give it to me, then.' And, snatching the hanger, she returned to the changing-room.

He was right, of course, she acknowledged grudgingly, surveying herself, her face flushed, her curls ruffled. It did suit her, the shade bringing her eyes and hair, her creamy skin hues to life, while the understated elegance of the coat-dress style enhanced her slenderness while at the same time giving her slim figure a rounded femininity.

The young woman knocked discreetly and entered. 'Oh, yes, *Señorita*. As Señor Torres said, it is perfect for you. But he wishes to see it, so please come.'

When she appeared Ramón was lounging in one of the small gilt chairs, entirely at ease, his hands clasped behind his head, and, gritting her teeth, she allowed herself to be walked up and down yet again. The whole performance, she thought bitterly, would be no more demeaning if he were some Moorish chieftain, giving the once-over to the latest slave addition to his harem.

As she turned on the carpet, she shot him a hostile glance from under her lashes. His face was an impassive mask but, as their eyes met, all at once, as never before in her life, she became acutely, hotly aware of her body under the soft silk of the dress. Beneath her smouldering resentment she felt her senses quicken in excitement, her leaping pulse-beat responding to what she felt in him, but even so, her gaze still locked with his, he cut through the twanging threads between them with a casual, 'She will take it,' and Georgia was able to escape back to the changing-room.

* * *

When she emerged, a pile of pink-wrapped packages were rested on one of the chairs and Ramón was just replacing his American Express card — nothing so vulgar as money ever changed hands in this establishment, she was quite sure.

He had been talking to the manager-ess and she was gazing up at him, eyes wide, a hypnotised rabbit beneath the highly polished sophistication. Georgia halted for a moment, unseen. You poor fool, she thought savagely, watching the shimmering expression on the woman's face, if you only knew. Any women unwise enough to stray into Ramón Torres's path he eats before breakfast, gobbles them up and crunches the bones.

She stared at them blankly, icy fingers tiptoeing up her spine at the image she had conjured up, but then he glanced round, saw her, and she had to force herself to walk across to him as he slid his wallet into his jacket pocket, not taking his eyes off her.

'Ready?' But without waiting for an answer he turned back to the young woman, said something to her, dropped his car keys on to the pile of pink packages and, putting a hand under Georgia's arm, led her out into the plaza.

'You shouldn't have bought me those things.' Too late, she felt she had to make a protest, however feeble.

Ramón gave a careless shrug. 'A few clothes? I can well afford them.'

'I'm sure you can,' she snapped, 'but that's not the point. Back in there, you

made it look exactly as if I was . . . '
Her voice died away.

'As if you were my mistress,' he put in, his voice softer and silkier than the pale maize dress. 'And would that be so unbearable?'

A brittle laugh spilled out. 'Yes — of course it would.' She must have spoken loudly, for several curious pairs of eyes turned to survey her. 'I shall never be any man's mistress — and you may as well accept that right now.'

'But I did not say that you would be *any* man's mistress.'

'And especially not yours.'

For a long moment, oblivious of the crowds jostling around them, they regarded one another, like two fencers seeking out their opponent's weakness — amber eyes, sparkling with mingled anger and apprehension, grey eyes, cool and inscrutable, remote even. But behind that very remoteness, the reserve with which he habitually cloaked himself, Georgia felt a dark, implacable force, felt it beating against her until her breathing quickened and she was all but panting. But then, without a word, he put his hand on her arm again and steered her through the milling crowd.

A boy was waiting, not alongside the Ferrari but in the driver's seat, the packages neatly stacked in the rear. When they appeared he scrambled out, still dreamy-eyed — no doubt, Georgia thought with half-amused sympathy, wrenched from his vision of himself as motor-racing champion of the world, taking yet another chequered flag. When Ramón dug in his pocket and proffered a generous tip, he accepted it with assumed nonchalance, then scampered off into the night.

Ramón handed her into her seat and she sank into the soft leather, grateful for the fact that he had to give all his attention to negotiating the still crowded streets, and then, as they left the town, for the darkness which enveloped them both . . .

* * *

The car glided to a halt outside the villa and Georgia climbed out, glancing as she did so at the luminous hands of the dashboard clock. Five minutes to midnight. She ought to feel exhausted — it had been a very long, emotionally fraught day — but somehow her body felt alert, vibrant even, the blood prickling along her veins, her nerve-ends twanging like softly plucked violin strings.

Midnight — the witching hour. Above their heads the moon was full and a million stars glittered against the indigo satin sky, while from below she could hear the restless hush of the sea as it rolled the little pebbles up and down the silver-grey beach.

Behind her she heard Ramón get out, then as she turned, she saw him, half in the shadow of a slender cypress tree, so that for a moment he looked unfamil-iar, half dark shadow, half silver moonlight. Unfamiliar? She'd known

177

this man for less than forty-eight hours, and yet already his body, his personality seemed to be imprinted on her, permeating her whole being so that he seemed as much a part of her as her own whorled fingerprints.

Half-shadow, half-moonlight — but wholly menacing. But then, as she stared at him, her mouth drying, he opened the rear door of the car and thrust some of the parcels at her.

'Take these in.'

She went into the house, still aware of him in every pore, her whole body receiving the tremor of the shock-wave when his arm brushed hers as he moved past her into her room. He switched on the wall-lights with his elbow, dropped the packages he was carrying on to a chair, took the rest from her and set them down as well.

The room seemed oppressive, the air heavy. Those peculiar feelings rippled through her again, screwing the tension in her even more, so that when he said, 'It's very close in here — would you like me to open a window?' she could do no more than mutter a 'please' in response to the casual remark.

He pulled back a pair of full-length blue-green velvet curtains, revealing double glass doors and a small balcony beyond. He threw open the doors, then turned to her.

'Thank you.' She was desperate now for him to go, and her tight features would barely stretch into a faint smile. 'It — it's cooler already.'

'But you are very pale.' He scrutinised her through slightly narrowed eyes. 'Come out and get some air.'

'I . . . ' She tried to say, All I want to do is go to sleep, but the words stuck fast in her throat, so instead she forced herself to walk stiffly out on to the balcony.

Below was the garden, with that same moonlit unfamiliarity which Ramón had had, its tiger stripes of black and silver harsh and uncompromising. He was standing behind her — she knew that without turning. He was not touching her, but she could feel him there, sense his body, even without the breath which stirred the curls on her neck and that scent of citrus, rising above the heady drift of perfume from a jasmine bush invisible in the darkness, and that far more elusive, far more potent scent which was Ramón — a scent which wove itself around her, creating strange, bewildering patterns in her brain.

It was making her dizzy, so that she took hold of the rail with both hands to steady herself, the metal cold against her clammy palms.

'Georgia.'

'Wh-what?' She did not — could not turn, for her life's sake.

'Georgia.'

And slowly she turned to face him.

'Come here.'

Still he made no effort to touch her, but that dark force was reaching out to her again, irresistible now, and she took a step towards him, then another, her legs heavy, as though she were wading through treacherous, clinging quicksand. And then, as he lifted his hands towards her, she knew that this was what she had been waiting for — was it only since yesterday? No, for her whole life she had waited for this moment.

In the intense moonlight she saw the pulse beating at the base of his throat. The faint movement beneath the tanned skin was erratic, hurried, as though to keep time with her own breathing from lungs which felt as if they were being painfully squeezed by a giant hand.

His fingers, as they closed over her shoulders, were warm. Even so, she shivered under their touch, but then, as he bent towards her, she lifted her face to his, her lips parting under the pressure of his mouth. His tongue thrust into her, claiming her sweetness in exchange for his own, ravaging every corner of the moist cavern until the stars reeled out of their orbits over her head.

His hands went from her shoulders,

sliding down her slender back, over her buttocks, pressing her to him, fitting her yielding flesh to his hard strength. She felt the fierce power run like a raging bush-fire from his loins into her body, so that it too was on fire with scorching heat.

With a broken little sound, part-sob, part-moan, she leaned against him, clinging to him, and Ramón, responding to her primitive, barely conscious appeal, caught her up in his arms. He held her, looking down at her for a moment, his eyes gleaming in the moonlight, then strode back through to her bedroom, laid her down on the aquamarine bedspread and came down beside her.

He ran his mouth down the side of her neck then fastened on that tell-tale pulse at the base, his lips slightly apart so that his tongue could flick back and forth across the crazily beating point until her breath was coming in rapid, shallow gasps. His hand closed over one neat breast, cupping its smallness in his palm, his thumb brushing across the nipple as it swelled against him, pleading for, demanding, more of his touch.

Slipping one shoulder-strap down her arm, he slid his hand into her neckline and drew out the pale, rose-tipped breast in its dainty half-cup bra. Easing it free, he lowered his head to take the pulsating centre deep inside his mouth, teasing at it with lips, teeth and tongue until she trembled and an intense shudder ran through her, shaking her whole frame as if it were a tree rocked by a winter gale. He lifted his head and looked at her, his eyes now dark and smoky with desire.

'Georgia — how beautiful you are. Your face, your body . . . '

His hands roved over her, so that through the soft fabric of her dress she felt the heat of his palm, caught the slightest tremor of his fingertips as they explored her as thoroughly as if she had been naked. And somehow that sensual exploration was even more arousing than it would have been if she had been naked, the slow friction of his palm against her flesh, warm skin against warm skin, with only the flimsy dress to keep them apart, almost unbearably erotic.

Over her breasts, her shoulders, her stomach, her thighs, his fingers moved, to rest at last, curled against that secret centre of her which throbbed and pulsed against his touch. With no conscious volition, she arched her body against him, and the unrestrained movement seemed to unleash something in him so that, with a muttered exclamation, he raised one hand to her neckline and tore the dress from her, ripping the fragile fabric away to reveal her slender curves, the tiny white briefs and bra.

Georgia heard his breath, harsh in his throat, then, half lifting herself, she tore at his shirt, tugging it free of the waistband until she could slide her hands inside. She ran first her fingers then the flat of her palm across his moist, smooth back, revelling in the feel of his muscles tautening and flexing beneath the skin as he moved towards her.

As he slid his hand down across her stomach once more, she thought, barely coherently, that she'd been wrong, totally wrong — it was far more erotic this way, with no barrier between them. Then, at the very moment when his fingers slipped inside her panties, another violent shudder shook her so that she closed her eyes and clutched convulsively at him, her nails scoring his back.

Easing himself away a fraction, he smiled down at her, his teeth gleaming very white in the half-light.

'Be patient, *mi pequeña cautiva* — my beautiful little captive.'

Little captive! Georgia went rigid with shock. Yes, that was what she was — that was how he saw her! Someone to be subdued, seduced, compelled into abject submission.

'No — no!'

Almost before her eyes, dazed and heavy as though from some powerful narcotic, could flutter open, she was fighting him, pushing him away.

'No — please, Ramón,' she whispered, a sob trapped in her throat. 'I — I can't — I don't want to.'

His whole body went tense, his fingers gripping her sides until she almost whimpered with pain. His eyes — the eyes of that minatory stranger in her hotel room — gazed down at her as though barely seeing her, and for a heart-stopping moment of sheer terror she thought that he was going to ignore her frantic pleas.

8

But then, even while Georgia lay helpless to save herself, Ramón thrust her away from him. As she rolled half on to her side, one arm up to shield her face, she heard his breathing, harsh and ragged, and, when she risked one fleeting glance, saw that his face was no longer flushed but very pale, while his eyes had narrowed into steel slits, like those of a jungle cat.

'You know, my sweet — ' the words were chipped from an Arctic glacier ' — you really shouldn't play those games.'

'Wh-what games?' Georgia could barely speak. 'I — '

'What games?' he echoed savagely, then jackknifed to his feet, as though to distance himself from her, and stood looking down at her, his mouth twisted with distaste. 'And for God's sake take that expression off your face.'

'Wh-what?' His words did not seem to penetrate her brain — only the raw fury in his voice.

'You almost had me fooled for a moment.' He was jamming his shirt back into his waistband. 'Lying there like some timid virgin.'

His venom bit deep, making her wince. 'But I — ' she began tremulously, but again he cut through her.

'I didn't realise that on top of all your other — skills you were such an accomplished little tease.'

'No, Ramón, I'm not!' Barely conscious of her near-nakedness, she scrambled to her knees. 'You must believe me. I'm s-sorry — so very sorry.'

'Sorry!' He ground out the word. 'You could have been a great deal sorrier, my dear.'

'What do you mean?'

'If you regularly play these games, sooner or later you'll come up against a lesser man than I — and then something very unpleasant will happen.' His fastidious lips curled.

'You — you mean — ?'

'Exactly — rape.' The word fell into the room with an ugly little sound and Georgia's flayed spirit shrank away from it. 'But perhaps that's the way you like it,' he went on scathingly. 'Maybe I was wrong — I should have ignored your sudden oh, so convincing act of maidenly modesty, your 'No — please, Ramón, I don't want to'.' Again he mimicked her. 'Is that what you really want, Georgia?'

Swooping down, he caught her by the arms, then dragged her upright so that their eyes were on a level, very close. When she tried to twist away, he put his hand up and wrenched her head back so that she was forced to face him.

'Is it?' He shook her slightly. 'Because I'm perfectly willing to oblige.'

'No — no, it isn't,' she whispered.

Just for a second his grip tightened even more, but then his lips thinned into a contemptuous sneer and he flung her back down across the bed.

'Women who use their bodies — '
and his chill eyes raked deliberately
over her, from her all but naked breasts
to the paleness of her thighs ' — must
sooner or later expect to pay the price.'

He stood gazing down at her, his
hands bunched at his sides, for what
seemed half an eternity. But his anger
was under control now, and there was
only icy indifference as he turned on his
heel and walked out of the room.

Georgia lay where he had flung her,
like a broken doll, her eyes wide but
unseeing, motionless save for one finger
plucking almost idly at a thread in the
coverlet. He hadn't struck her, she
thought with a strange, disembodied
sense of calm. He hadn't harmed a hair
of her head, but she could hardly have
felt worse if he had carried out his
threat and physically violated her.

Somewhere in the house a door
banged and as the sound registered she
tensed in every limb, but then there was
silence. She found she was shivering

violently, icy cold although the room still felt very hot, and with a tremendous effort of will she forced herself off the bed and, like some kind of automaton, went through to the bathroom.

She did not switch the light on — the thought of what she would see in the mirror made her flayed spirit cringe — but in the filtering moonlight set the shower running and stepped under its cascade. She scrubbed at herself, but though the water warmed her chill body it could not wipe off the feel of his hands on her flesh, nor erase the memory of his searing contempt from her brain.

Still moving mechanically, she dried herself, went back to the bedroom and put her nightdress on. Just as she was switching off the wall-lights, she saw the sliver of black dress lying in a tangled heap at the foot of the bed. With her toe, she thrust it out of sight, then, as reaction finally set in, she collapsed back on to the bed and, huddling herself into a tight little ball, lay staring into the darkness, her knuckles pressed to her mouth.

When she roused, daylight instead of moonlight was streaming in through the half-closed shutters. Someone had been in: a tray of tea, now lukewarm, stood on the bedside table, and when she raised herself on one elbow she saw that her parcels had gone.

Then, what she had been trying to hold at bay — remembrance of the previous night — flooded in and she dropped back on to the pillow again. She squeezed her eyes shut in a vain attempt to blot out the room, and the memories. But the images — of her lying in his arms, of his face, that dusky flush along the cheekbones, of his eyes, warm and smoke-grey with passion, of his dark head lying across her breast — could not be wiped away. Images, images . . . And sensations, too — his hands roving over her trembling, avid body, his lips, his teeth fastening over her swelling nipples . . .

Georgia realised that her breath was coming faster, in quick, shallow gasps, and, opening her eyes, she saw with horror, through the thin cotton of her nightie, the centre of her breasts begin to tauten and harden, as though treacherously yearning for his mouth again.

With a groan, wrenched from the very depths of her being, she rolled over on to her side, staring at the wall. How could she have done it? Over and over, the question thundered in her ears as a red, burning tide of shame swept through her, uncheckable. How could she have laid herself open to such — such humiliation, such degradation?

Had she been very slightly drunk? Was that why she'd behaved so out of character — so like the woman he thought her? Drunk, on two small glasses of white wine? Oh, come on, Georgy, an inner voice mocked her, you'll have to think of a better one than that.

As for Ramón, she could hardly

blame him for his reaction. If he thought her a sexually mature woman — a hysterical little laugh bubbled up, but she forced it down — then to him it would also seem that she was — what had he called her? — a tease, leading him on, advancing to the very brink then coolly calling a halt exactly when she wished.

But then, in the midst of her despair, the beginnings of a saving anger stirred in her. How dared he assume *anything* at all about her? It was his arrogance, his chauvinism — the lordly male presuming that all women were as experienced as he, ready and willing for any man who deigned to notice them. No man — except her adored brother — had ever been allowed to become really close to her, but was that it? Were all of the species carbon copies — even if pale ones — of Ramón Torres? Very probably . . .

But she couldn't lie here all day, pondering on arrogant, unfeeling swine — or one of them would be in here very soon, no doubt, to drag her out.

Flinging back the sheet, she went across to the wardrobe. When she slid it open, she saw hanging beside her own few clothes the outfits he had bought her. There was the maize coat-dress, the taupe linen skirt with its little matching jacket, and a blouse in heavy white cotton, edged with crunchy hand-worked lace. The blue and white striped dress hung next to it — the one which had looked like a piece of discarded, old-fashioned mattress-cover until she had stepped into it and it had become a shift dress, its chic, elegant lines perfectly setting off her long, slender limbs. And here were the two skirts in swirling, exotic patterns, and a jade wrap-over top in cotton jersey to go with either.

Georgia's hand wandered slowly across them one by one, her fingers softly caressing each in turn. Which should she wear this morning — one of the skirts, or perhaps the shift dress? Her fingers hesitated over it then were withdrawn, suddenly, as if it had burned them. She wasn't going to wear *any* of his clothes — the clothes he'd forced on her in that boutique, in that other show of male dominance versus female submission. She hadn't yielded last night — the bull had stood up to the matador, had been brought to its knees in the blood-stained sand of the arena, but had not surrendered — so she certainly wasn't going to give in over this.

With a little spurt of exultation, she swept the clothes along to the far end of the rail and got out instead one of her own outfits — a pale lemon-sherbet blouse and white cotton skirt.

At one end of the wardrobe was a row of drawers, where the maid had placed her underwear the previous day. She pulled one out, looking for a clean bra and pants, and heard herself gasp as she stared down at a drawer full not of simple white cotton undies, but of exquisite lingerie. Her hands all at once unsteady, she picked up the topmost piece. It was a delicate little half-bra, a froth of cream silk and lace, and beneath were a matching camisole top, teddy, and tiny, lace-ruffled panties, with minute satin bows at the thigh.

There was another set, this time in palest, sea-green satin and lace, so lovely, so cobweb-fragile, that for a moment Georgia's eyes filled with foolish tears at its sheer perfection. At one side was a silk nightdress and matching négligé in soft amber, a shade which, surely, exactly matched her eyes.

She held up the nightdress, letting it fall in soft, shimmering folds to her toes, then picked up the cream half-bra again and held it against her. It cupped her small breasts perfectly — in fact everything, down to the suspender-belts and silk stockings, was in her size. They were intended for her, no one else . . .

Of course — while she was in the changing-room that last time, the manageress must have assembled them under Ramón's swift instructions. But what must she have thought — and the maid who had unpacked them this morning? Precisely — that she was his mistress, his latest conquest. And most likely an even easier one than most, she thought savagely. Slamming the drawer closed, she snatched open the next, where her own few undies lay neatly stacked, and, pulling out her plainest bra and pants, she threw them on to the bed.

Although the curtains were still drawn, the maid must have half opened the full-length glass doors, for as Georgia went towards the bathroom she caught faint sounds from outside. Pushing the doors fully open, she stepped softly out on to the balcony and cautiously looked down. There was no one to be seen in the garden, though on the terrace almost directly beneath her a table had been set for breakfast — for two, she couldn't help registering — and, almost invisible behind a screen of conifers and tangled hibiscus and bougainvillaea, she saw for the first time one segment of a blue-tiled swimming-pool.

It came again, that faint splash, then

the next instant she saw Ramón. He was coming down the pool in a rapid crawl, his tanned shoulders cleaving the blue water, scything effortlessly through it. He reached the end, ducked under the water so that he was a blurred outline as he twisted like a seal, then surfaced five yards down and vanished from her view. Moments later he reappeared but this time, instead of turning, he hauled himself out and padded across to a lounger, where a towel had been tossed down.

The water lay in glistening droplets on his glossy skin, as silky as the pelt of an animal. He was wearing the minutest of black trunks, slung low on his hips, and as he bent to retrieve the towel she could not help but see the neat, taut muscles of his buttocks, the top of the cleft between them visible above the line of his trunks.

When he turned, towelling his dark head, her eyes travelled slowly over his shoulders and powerful chest, with its crisp black hairs. A tiny diamond of water, caught among them, escaped and rolled slowly down his stomach, catching the light as it did so. She watched it course down the horizontal ridges of muscle, across his belly, then, as it disappeared against his trunks, others ran down across his thighs to catch in the web of hairs there before dropping to the tiles.

He blotted himself roughly dry then, as Georgia stood there unable to move a muscle, he turned away from her towards the lounger, peeled off the trunks and caught up a pair of denim shorts. She wanted to escape — wanted to turn and run — but instead, clinging to the rail for support, just as she had done the previous night, she stared down at that superb body, her breathing coming fast and shallow again, a bead of sweat trickling down her back.

Only when he zipped up the shorts, thrust his feet into a pair of rope-soled espadrilles and picked up the towel did she finally manage to rouse herself, dragging her clammy hands from the rail and flinging herself away from the balcony-edge just as he swung round in her direction.

She heard his firm footsteps coming up the shallow flight of steps, then silence — except for the rasp of her uneven breath and the irregular pounding of her heart. She leaned up against the wall beside the glass door, her hands splayed, afraid that without their slight support her knees would give way beneath her.

Now she knew the terrible truth. In spite of her anger, her shame — yes, her fear of him, even — she wanted Ramón physically, as she had wanted no other man.

Her hand pressed to her mouth, she stood staring out across the garden to the mountains beyond, until she heard footsteps again — on the terrace now — a maid's voice and Ramón's greeting in reply.

Down in the hall, a black-haired, smartly dressed woman of about fifty, who introduced herself as Rosalia,

Señor Torres's housekeeper, met her and took her out to the terrace, where the table had been moved into the shade of a wisteria-clad pergola. Ramón, in a pale blue T-shirt and the denim shorts, just about glanced up, grunting something that might almost have been '*Buenos días*' as the woman pulled out the chair opposite to him and Georgia, composed now, after that appalling revelation, but very pale, slid into it.

As the housekeeper flicked a few imaginary crumbs from the pristine white cloth then turned away, he raised his eyes again. She had braced herself for this moment but there was nothing — no anger in them, no contempt, no scorn — nothing. They were cool, impersonal chips of ice.

'Help yourself. And if there is anything else you wish, Rosalia will fetch it for you.' And he turned back to the notebook at his elbow, in which he had been scribbling.

'Th — thank you.'

She'd thought, up there in the

bedroom, that she'd finally won the battle with herself — the battle to be aloof, calm, controlled — but now, to her horror, she heard the weak tremor in her voice. Somehow, though, she had to get matters back to their former sparring relationship.

'What's that you're drinking?' A jug of fresh orange, its icy coldness smoking in the warm air, had been set beside her, but a half-empty glass with a darker liquid stood by his plate.

'Tomato juice. Do you want some? I thought you would prefer orange, but — '

'Oh, no, thanks — orange is fine.' She paused, then, before her courage could totally desert her, added, 'I just wondered if it might be tiger's blood.'

For the first time that morning he really looked at her, a long, considering scrutiny, then, 'No — just tomato juice.' And, leaving her feeling as if yet again she'd come off second-best, he returned to his book.

Georgia poured herself some orange,

then took a croissant and tried to eat it, carefully dividing all her attention between her plate and a terracotta pot of scarlet geraniums near by. But as the silence between them continued her inner tension grew, so that when a sudden little breeze rustled the climbing jasmine behind her and sent a shower of tiny white flower-heads scattering across the table she jumped at the almost soundless sound they made.

It was the same jasmine which had filled her balcony with such heady, overpowering perfume the previous night. Did he remember? She looked up, in the same instant as Ramón's eyes were raised; their gazes locked, then hers slid confusedly away.

He drained his coffee-cup and got to his feet, as though all at once anxious to be away from her. But then, after pushing in his chair, he stood leaning his hands on it, looking down at her once more.

'The equipment you ordered has

been delivered. It has been put in my office, ready for you to begin work.'

Deliberately, Georgia poured herself a cup of coffee and stirred in cream. 'Oh, I should have told you earlier. I've decided not to take the job.'

Her eyes were still on the circle of cream — she could not lift them — and her fingers tightened on the coffee-spoon, but when he spoke his voice was perfectly even.

'How easily I am coming to under-stand you, my sweet. I somehow thought that this would be your reaction. But you see, you agreed, and I intend to hold you to that.'

'No, I did not agree.' She looked up now, glaring into his expressionless face. 'I merely said I *might*, and now I've changed my mind. Sorry.'

She lifted her coffee but then, as Ramón came round the small table to her, set it down again quickly.

'Georgia . . . ' he rested his hands over her wrist, without any pressure, but she received the warning message loud and clear ' . . . I wish you to prepare those plans for me — and therefore you will. I have already rung the architects — you need to meet them, of course, to pool your ideas — and they are flying down from Madrid.'

She expelled an angry breath. 'You really are a bastard — you know that?'

'Of course,' he replied coolly. 'You are not the first, by any means, to come up with such an original term of endearment.' There was a slight pause then, 'All your materials are ready,' he said. 'You may work in my office — and if you need to go out on to the site my foreman will provide you with a protective hat.'

He removed his hand and she stared down at the crumbs on her plate. He was standing just behind her, but out of the corner of her eye she could see him — see the strong, tanned legs and thighs, the sun glinting on the little hairs where they disappeared under the edge of his shorts . . .

It just wasn't fair, she thought despairingly, that he had this extra weapon — this hold that his body had over her. She really ought to refuse, tell him where he could put his job — and himself. But she was trapped here, with no hope of release until Grant came, so at least this would give her an excuse for shutting herself away from him, working all day — and all night too, perhaps — to get the plans finished. This way, too, she might stand a chance of filling her brain with ideas other than those treacherous thoughts which were threatening to take over her mind completely . . .

'All right.' She did not look up at him.

He picked up his notebook, stuffing it into the pocket of his shorts. 'I shall want you to have a full set of preliminary sketches ready for them.'

'Of course,' she replied, with a touch of hauteur. 'There's no need to teach me my job, I assure you. When are they coming?'

'This afternoon.'

'This — ' She had been determined to hold her reactions in check, but this was too much. 'But I — ' She broke off again, biting her lip. *Somehow* those sketches would be ready or she, Georgia Leigh, would have expired in the attempt. 'Very well.'

Her voice was brittle-edged, like glass, but he merely nodded coolly. All along he'd never had any doubt, of course. Please let me, she thought, just once in my life, dent his arrogant self-assurance very, very slightly. Then she pushed back her chair.

'In that case I'd better get started, hadn't I?' she said sweetly, and stalked past him, head held high, back into the villa.

★   ★   ★

'*Adiós, adiós.*'

Georgia breathed an inward sigh of relief as the tail-lights of the hired Mercedes disappeared round the corner. Although it meant that she and Ramón were alone again, she'd been glad that Señores Gonzalez and Herrera had refused his invitation to stay overnight, or even for dinner. At least this way she'd be spared several hours of polite small talk, coming on top of such an exhausting day — a day which, even so, she knew inside herself had gone well.

It hadn't got off to a particularly promising start, though. She'd been in the office, the remains of a snatched lunch still on a tray at her side, when, after just a perfunctory knock, Ramón had put his head in to inform her curtly that the architects were here. 'Oh, and wear one of the outfits I bought you.'

She'd muttered something under her breath along the lines of, 'Yes, sir, no, sir, three bags full, sir,' but the door was already closed.

Twenty minutes later, as she was crossing the hall, the sitting-room door had opened and Ramón had emerged. He'd halted when he'd caught sight of her and allowed himself a leisurely head-to-toe perusal of the taupe linen suit and white blouse.

'Well, will I do?' Her inner tension had put a snap in her voice.

His eyes had lingered on her a moment longer.

'Just one slight improvement.' And, before she could move, he'd undone the top button of her blouse, easing the neckline slightly apart.

The two grey-suited men had greeted her with a mixture of condescension and barely veiled hostility. They'd clearly regarded her as Ramón's latest plaything, being foisted on them as a reward for her favours, but this had only stiffened her resolve to show them how wrong they were. And at the same time, she'd thought with a bitter little twist, she might even convince Ramón that, however useless she might be in bed, at least he'd hired himself a first-class designer.

It hadn't helped, of course, that he'd insisted on sitting in on all the discussions — to translate, he'd told her blandly, even though the architects' English was impeccable. They'd toured the site together, then gone through her sketches in minute detail, closely questioning her on her ideas, feeding in thoughts of their own, some of which she'd agreed to take on board, so that now — it was nearly nine o'clock, she registered with astonishment — she was feeling like a wrung-out rag. But through the long day she'd sensed a subtle change in the men's attitude, and now they were going off seemingly satisfied that the landscaping was not, after all, in the hands of Ramón's current incompetent bimbo.

She stood for a moment, her hand still half raised in farewell, then glanced round at Ramón, despising herself yet at the same time willing him to smile at her, say, Well done, that was a great performance you gave in there.

All he did say, though, was, 'I'm going down to the beach for a swim before dinner. Want to come?'

What she wanted was to take herself

off to bed, not even bothering with dinner, but maybe this was the nearest this haughty reserved man could get to expressing his approval, so perhaps she shouldn't reject this brusque olive-branch.

'Good idea,' she replied brightly. 'I'll go and change.'

When she came back down, wearing her dayglo lilac one-piece swimsuit under her T-shirt and shorts, he was waiting in the hall below and she paused at the curve of the staircase, suddenly frozen into immobility. He was dressed in a navy robe, a towel slung over one shoulder. The loosely belted robe hung open, revealing a long, tapering V of tanned chest, while his legs were bare, his feet thrust into espadrilles.

He was propping himself against a carved wooden chest, his arms folded, his dark head bent, so that she could only just catch the morose scowl on his face as he stared down at the floor, lost in his thoughts. There was nothing different about him — even the scowl was the one she had seen a hundred times before, black brows drawn down over those wonderful eyes — and yet Georgia all at once was staring down at him as though she had never set eyes on him in her life before.

Around her, the world seemed to pull itself up by its roots, lurch, endlessly tilt sideways then very slowly right itself. But in one blinding moment she knew with perfect clarity that she herself would never be quite the same again, because, for the first time in her life — and the last, she knew that just as clearly — she had fallen in love. She loved Ramón.

But she couldn't! It was too terrible . . . She gazed at her hands, clutching at the wooden balustrade, saw the knuckles whiten, the bones stand out taut beneath the skin.

Almost overwhelmed by her emotions, she looked up, just as Ramón, roused perhaps by some slight movement of hers, raised his eyes and saw her. For one fragile moment it was as if the still air between them were full of noise and clamour, then somehow — she never knew how — she straightened herself and went on down the stairs.

'Ready?' He levered himself upright.

'Yes.'

Awareness of him was in every pore of her skin, and, terrified that his cat's senses would pick up her turmoil, her glance slid past his and she walked to the door. She had crossed the terrace when, without warning, he gripped her wrist.

'What?'

She swung round sharply, fearful that even by touching her he might fathom her secret.

'Wait a moment.' Digging in his robe pocket, he produced a torch and flicked in on. 'The path is very steep.'

Before she could draw back he took her hand, his grip tightening as she tensed, so that she was forced to let him lead her. Only the path ahead was illuminated — they themselves were all but invisible, so that when she gave him a sidelong glance all she could see was a dark profile, hard-edged against the night sky. But the feel of his hand, warm and strong as it enveloped hers, and, his thigh against hers, was setting up powerful vibrations inside her body.

The steep path widened, and as the torch lit the pale sand of the beach his grasp eased a fraction so that she was able to snatch her hand free with a muttered, 'I can manage now, thanks.'

'Good.' The faintest irony underscored the word.

At the line which marked the division of wet and dry sand she dropped her towel and quickly peeled off her T-shirt and shorts. Conscious of the high-cut line of the swimsuit which made her legs, pale silver in the moonlight, look endless, she waded out and flung herself into the dark opaque water, letting it close around her, tingling-cool.

Out of the corner of her eye, though, she was watching as Ramón shed his wrap and plunged into the sea, cutting swiftly past her through the waves until she could make out only the occasional glint of moonlight on his shoulders as they broke the surface.

But he turned for the shore at last, and she too made for the beach, where, snatching up her towel, she began hastily scrubbing at herself. When he arrived she was wrapped in it, still in her wet swimsuit.

'Aren't you going to change out of that?'

He picked up his own towel and briefly rubbed his hair before starting on his chest.

'No, I won't bother.' She couldn't tell him that she'd forgotten her underwear and didn't want to put on just the T-shirt and shorts.

'You'll be cold.'

'N-no — I'm fine,' she said, through teeth which were beginning to chatter, though only in part from the cold.

Dropping his towel on to the sand, he very deliberately put his hands on her bare shoulders.

'Georgia,' he said softly.

Terrified that he would feel her love reaching out to him, she strove desperately to put up a barrier in her mind against his searching gaze. But his touch felt warm against her chill flesh — it must have been the sheer animal energy of the man — and suddenly, without a moment's warning, the touch of his skin against hers set all her pulses flickering crazily, so that when he bent his head towards her she lifted her face, her lips parting to receive his kiss.

It was gentle at first but deepened rapidly, and as his tongue thrust against hers she gave a strangled moan and, fingers tangling in his hair, pressed him closer until she felt the imprint of his teeth on her lips.

Her whole body was on fire, ablaze as, aching with love, she opened her arms to him. This time, she all at once knew with a dazzling joy, there would be no fear, no timorous holding back. Whatever came of tonight was right. She would give herself to him eagerly, willingly — lovingly.

The sand was cold beneath them as they slipped to their knees. On the very edge of consciousness, she felt his skilful hands peel her wet swimsuit from her, felt his warmth against her, the power of him as Ramón held her hard against him, her soft body yielding to his strength.

When he lowered his head to her breasts to suckle them, she made small, incoherent sounds as she fell back across his arm, her hair brushing the sand. His mouth went lower, his tongue circling in her navel, and she threshed restlessly as he held her, her hips grasped in his hands. And when his searching lips moved lower still she arched wildly against him as tumultuous little sobs were torn from her throat.

'Please, Ramón . . .'

Her voice was slurred with desire, her

fingers twining again and again in his hair, and he raised his head to look at her. In the half-dark his face was a shuttered mask, but his eyes were very pale, almost luminous, as with one hand he turned her to him.

'What is it you want, *querida*?' His voice was a soft caress and she muttered something unintelligible against his palm. 'Do you want me to make love to you, Georgia? Do you?'

He lightly brushed his other hand across the top of her thighs, sending spasms of sensation so exquisite that they were almost like pain shooting through her.

Beyond all rational thought, she heard herself cry out, 'Yes — oh, yes, Ramón. You know I do.' And snatching at his hand, still lying against her face, she buried her lips in the palm.

Next instant, the hand was dragged free and she felt herself thrust roughly away from him.

'Good. I'm so glad.'

Drowning in sensation, she could

barely surface, but her eyes fluttered then opened, to see him calmly getting to his feet.

'Ramón!' The whimper of anguish was wrenched from her but, reaching for his robe, he barely glanced at her.

'What is it?'

'I — I thought you w-wanted to make love to me.'

There was a long silence. He stood coolly looking down at her as she lay at his feet, too shattered even to care about her nakedness, then said, 'I may have wanted you — in the purely physical sense of a man for any halfway attractive woman — but nothing more.' He paused, then came the final killing thrust. 'You see, my sweet. I don't make love to women I despise.'

'But — why?' she faltered.

'Why lead you on just as you led me last night? Oh, that's simple enough — little teases, my sweet, need to be taught a lesson.' His voice flicked at her raw spirit like a light whiplash. 'I think I have taught you that lesson — and yet you still want me, don't you?'

From somewhere she summoned the tattered rags of her pride. 'No. No, I don't.'

But her lips quivered, and with a little laugh he came down beside her on his haunches.

'Oh, but you do, *amada mia*.' His voice mocked her. 'Don't lie to me — or to yourself.'

As she flinched, he raised his hand to run his fingers with deliberate slowness across her breasts, and instantly they sprang up beneath his touch, yearning, supplicating. As she bit on her inner mouth until she felt the salt taste of blood, he dropped his hand with a contemptuous gesture and straightened up. When he went to lift her to her feet, though, she pulled clear of him. 'Leave me alone, damn you.'

'Oh, dear. Sulking because you can't get your own way? But I did warn you, *querida* — ' his voice hardened from its silky purr ' — that you weren't strong enough to stand against me, and that I would bend your will to mine.'

Yes, but you didn't warn me not to fall in love with you, did you? The desolate words echoed and re-echoed in her mind.

'Well, are you coming?' There was a note of impatience in his voice now. 'I have work to do before dinner.'

'Not yet.'

'As you wish.' He gave a casual half-lift of one shoulder, then next moment the torch landed beside her. 'I shall see you later, then.'

Pride, only stubborn pride, when what she really longed to do was to lie down on the wet sand and die, kept her rigidly upright as he sauntered off across the beach. She watched as he rounded a clump of oleander bushes, heard his footsteps on the stony path, then all sound faded except the shush-shush of the sea. Just beside her a little wave ran up, almost to her feet, and she watched it as if from very far away. Of course, she should have known that a man like Ramón would need revenge — would need it and take it. Strange — she'd been on her guard all day and then, loving him, she'd allowed that guard to slip. Loving him . . . Oh, God, what had she done?

Another wave came. She watched this one as well then, barely conscious of the cold, huddled on the sand like some wounded sea-animal which had dragged itself to the water's edge to die, and the pain and humiliation spurted through her like evil-tasting bile.

9

Hmm. Pencil poised, Georgia pursed her lips in intense thought. Should the final drop from the stream to the pool be a sheer fall, dramatic by day and even more so at night, when floodlit? Or should she bring the water down in a series of smaller, rock-strewn cascades — less of the drama but very pretty, if she lined the banks with ferns and water-plants? She might even —

Oh, what did it matter anyway? The pencil slipped from her fingers and rolled unnoticed across the drawing-board and on to the floor. She would never see the finished creation, never cross that ornamental little bridge she'd laboured so hard over yesterday, never dabble her fingers in that pretty little fountain, never sit in the tree-lined shade of the tiny plaza . . .

Others would — someone else, one

day, would stroll hand in hand with Ramón down through the curving alleys, past the pool to the beach below. Someone else . . .

The square-lined paper in front of her shimmered and blurred, but then, drawing a deep breath, she retrieved her pencil and bent over the board once more . . .

★　★　★

'Oh.' With no warning, the set-square was removed from her fingers and she looked up to meet Ramón's eyes, shuttered and impassive as ever. Just for a moment her insides did their too familiar plunge, then righted themselves as she said, 'Yes, did you want something?'

Her cool, impersonal tone provoked a tiny frown between the elegant black brows, but all he said was, 'To tell you, for the third time this evening, that dinner is ready — as it has been for the past half-hour.'

'Oh, I'm sorry. Please apologise to Rosalia — ' she wouldn't allow him to mar her good manners ' — but tell her I'm not hungry. A sandwich will do for me — in here, please.'

The frown deepened infinitesimally. 'As on the last three evenings, you mean? I'm sorry, but Rosalia is becoming distressed. She thinks you do not like her cooking.'

'But you know it isn't — '

'And as her family has been in the service of my family for generations — to say nothing of the fact that she is an excellent cook — you will dine tonight.'

'Look, I'm sorry — but I'm really not hungry.'

He shrugged. 'A glass of sherry will improve your appetite.' And, abruptly pulling back her chair, he lifted her to her feet.

She put a hand to her head, dizzy suddenly from the hours of concentrated mental effort, and as she stood swaying she instinctively flung up her hands to steady herself against the nearest solid object — his chest. Fingers spread, she could feel just under his breastbone the strong beat of his heart. It was the first time since that appalling night on the beach that he had touched her, or she him, and now she was shaken to her roots by the feel of him under her hands. When she looked up into his face, it was the first time too, it seemed, that their eyes had done more than skate past each other.

For three or four of those strong heartbeats they gazed at one another and then, in precisely the same instant that Ramón, with an odd little grimace, stepped back, she drew her hands away as if they burned.

As he went out, without another glance, Georgia stood leaning against the desk, watching him. Who were they kidding, she thought savagely, those poets who rhapsodised over the joys of love? Love was a terrible thing. It was a sharp, physical pain, a dragging ache in the guts which you were never free from, a dreary emptiness which the whole world couldn't fill.

Her shoulders were sagging. She straightened them and followed him out to the terrace . . .

★   ★   ★

'More coffee?'

As Ramón picked up the silver coffee-pot, she gave his left shoulder a polite, empty smile. 'No, thank you.'

'And no cognac?'

She shook her head, watching as he poured some of the amber liquid into his glass, swirled it round almost absently, then tossed it down. His head was tilted so that she was aware of the strong lines of his throat, the slight movement of the muscles as he swallowed. As she stared, fascinated, he went to set down the empty glass and their glances met once more, his eyes looking deep into hers. There was no wind this evening, not even a breath, yet somehow for an instant it seemed to

Georgia that the air was full of a rushing gale which snatched her up, whirled her wildly about then set her down on the zinnia-patterned cushion of her patio chair, not a copper curl out of place though her breathing was flurried.

'There is a fiesta tonight in one of the mountain villages,' he remarked off-handedly. 'Nothing spectacular but it is genuine — not put on twice-weekly for the benefit of tourists. You will enjoy it.'

'You're quite sure of that, are you?' Her mouth closed with a snap on the last word.

'Of course.'

She darted him a resentful glance. This was more like the old Ramón; for the last three days he'd behaved with a scrupulously polite formality which would have frozen her if she'd allowed it to, but now here was the arrogant assumption that she would go to this fiesta — and enjoy herself when she got there.

'Actually,' she said coolly, 'I thought

I'd have another early night.' Of staring at the ceiling — or, as a change of view, the bedroom wall — until dawn began to filter through her curtains . . .

'There's no need to dress up,' he went on exactly as if she had not spoken. 'It will be a very simple village occasion.'

'You mean a frog T-shirt occasion?' she enquired waspishly.

'Not exactly.' His voice was perfectly even. 'But I am sure you will find something suitable.'

Left alone, Georgia stared unseeingly at the small posy of clove carnations in the centre of the table, lit by two candle-lamps. What was happening to her? she thought miserably. She should have banged the table, shouted, I'm not going — and there's nothing you can do about it, you — you overbearing, chauvinistic tyrant. But now, instead of standing up to him — like the old Georgia Leigh — she'd go without another word, she knew that, because it meant that she'd be with him for a few more precious hours. And if that was what love did — make you weak and clinging and vulnerable — then the sooner she shook herself free of this folly — no, this madness — the better it would be.

Up in her room, she showered quickly, flexing the muscles of her back and shoulders which were cramped from hours of close work, then padded across to the wardrobe. Serve him right if she did wear the frog. She half lifted the T-shirt out then saw, hanging at the far end of the rail, those other clothes . . .

When she went back down he was waiting on the terrace, sitting at the now cleared table and staring at the flowers as she had done. He too had changed — he was wearing a white shirt and dark grey cords, and across the back of his chair was slung a big black cashmere cardigan.

A moth, attracted by the light, came blundering towards a candle-lamp and he gently brushed it away. It returned, he pushed it away again, but then a third time, before he could prevent it, the creature flew down into the glass globe, fluttered crazily as it felt the scorching heat of the candle then fell, dying.

And that's how it will be for me, Georgia thought with a sudden stab of fear. If I don't fight it, I'll be destroyed, just like that poor moth — consumed in the flames of my love for Ramón.

At that moment he glanced up and saw her standing in the shadows, and she forced herself to walk forward into the light. His cool eyes surveyed her, taking in the silky blue-green skirt, its clever bias cut rippling out to emphasise the slim line of her hips, and the way the jade cotton jersey top clung to her, making the most of her slight curves.

'If you're quite ready,' he said curtly, and walked down the steps to the car.

Only then, as the ridiculous disappointment welled in her, did she realise how she had been holding her breath, waiting for his reaction. In spite of her resolve, she'd come downstairs, her heart pitter-pattering, a little glow on her face, but that had all gone . . .

★　★　★

The village was tucked snugly into the mountains, most of its whitewashed houses overlooking dizzying drops to the valley, dark apart from where pale orange chinks of light showed from the little farmsteads.

Ramón, whose longest speech since driving away from the villa had been a stream of Spanish invective directed against a driver who had been mis-guided enough to stray in front of him, parked and led the way up a narrow, cobbled alley between high white-washed walls, over which drifted the night-time scent of flowers.

Ahead she heard music, and as they turned a corner into the crowded village plaza she saw, grouped on a makeshift platform alongside the stone façade of the church, a band. Fairy-lights were strung from the plane trees which lined the square, and trestle-tables of food and wine had been set up. A dance was just ending, and as the laughter and applause rippled Ramón collected two glasses of red wine and led her to a table near the back.

A youngish woman in black, with a guitar, came forward to the front of the band, to raucous cheers and foot-stamping.

'Who is she?' Georgia whispered.

'Ana Bautista — she's a well-known local folk-singer.'

The woman strummed a few notes and began to sing. She had an attractive, husky, rather plaintive voice, well-suited to the style of the song, and Georgia, who could not understand a word of it, found to her horror that tears were stinging her eyes. To cover her discomfiture, she took a few sips of the wine.

'What was it about?'

Ramón, who was joining in the

applause with enthusiasm, turned his cool eyes on her.

'Oh, the usual thing.' He grimaced slightly. 'Young love, illict love, unrequited love.'

'I see.' Well, she, Georgia Leigh, could get up on the stage and sing about the last of those loves, she thought forlornly, and buried her nose in the wine. It had a rough, almost harsh edge to it which somehow matched her mood tonight.

When the next song ended, she said rather tautly, 'More unrequited love, I suppose?'

'No.' In the soft light, Ramón's eyes were very pale. 'It was based on an old Spanish proverb.'

'Really?' she replied brightly. 'Too many cooks spoil the broth, you mean?'

'Not quite.' The saturnine face looked back at her across the narrow table. 'More along the lines of take anything you want — take it and pay for it.'

'Oh.' The empty smile slipped from

her face; the chill little aphorism held something — not exactly menacing, but profoundly disturbing.

A male act followed the singer — a comic, to judge from the gales of laughter, Georgia decided as she sat, a polite grin fixed into place. Ramón wasn't laughing, but from time to time she saw his thin lips twitch with wry amusement.

He caught her glance and, leaning towards her, said, 'He is giving all us men advice on how to enjoy ourselves — how do you say? — on the side, while ensuring our docile little wives don't do the same.'

'Oh, I see.' Drawing back slightly, she added spikily, 'How very amusing for you all.'

After the acts, the band struck up again and couples made their way on to the small dance area.

'Would you like to dance?'

Georgia turned as Ramón spoke. His face wore that aloof mask which she had grown so accustomed to. He didn't

want to dance with her, she knew that
— he was only going through the
motions of the attentive host — but she
heard herself say, 'Yes, please, I'd love
to.'

For a second, that muscle flicked in
the corner of his mouth, then he
pushed back his chair and led her
through the crowded tables.

As a waltz began, he took her in his
arms. She thought that he must be as
tinglingly aware as she was of the last
time he had done so — the image of
them lying at the edge of the sea was so
vivid in her mind that surely it must
spill over into his. But when she risked
a glance up into his face, lit from above
by a row of lights which threw his
cheekbones into relief while shadowing
his eyes, she could catch nothing of his
mood.

Her own face, she thought with
sudden bitterness, was so transparent,
so revealing, that even now, after days
of keeping her emotions in cold storage,
she couldn't be sure that he didn't

237

guess at least some of her feelings for him. And despise her even more, she added miserably.

But then, as Ramón's arms enclosed her once more, she tried to shake herself clear of her unhappy mood. Perhaps — no, certainly — he would never hold her like this again, and all the rest of her life she would have to struggle to keep alive the memory of this one dance. For years that memory would be bitter, then bittersweet, then finally maybe comforting — something very special that she could take out and look at when she was alone.

Closing her eyes, she surrendered to the moment, the feel of his body as the muscles tensed to lead her through the maze of dancers, his hand resting in the small of her back, his head bent slightly towards her so that his cheek was brushing softly against her hair and she could smell his citrus aftershave. And gradually she became filled with a numb despair.

When the dance ended they drew

apart, not joining in the applause, and stared at each other. But as the band struck up again he asked, his voice wholly neutral, 'Another dance?'

'No, I don't — '

'Ramón. Ramón Torres.' A heavily built man had got up from among a group of men at one of the tables near by and was clapping him on the back, launching into a torrent of Spanish.

Ramón disentangled himself and made perfunctory introductions. 'Señorita Leigh, Carlos Vergara.'

The man took her hand, bowed low over it then kissed it in an old-fashioned gesture. '*Encantada, Señorita.*'

'*Señor,*' she smiled.

He said something to Ramón, who hesitated, then turned to Georgia. 'Excuse me for a moment while I talk with Carlos and his friends. I have not seen them for several years, and you will be bored.'

'More men's jokes, you mean?' she asked, her voice brittle.

'Perhaps,' he replied evenly, 'but

more because they do not speak English so will be unable to talk to you.' He was turning away, then paused and put his hand on her arm. 'Wait for me at our table.' And don't dare try anything while my back's turned — that was the clear message from the fingers digging slightly into her flesh.

But she merely smiled blandly and said, 'Of course.'

She was making her way through the throng when her path was blocked by a young man in jeans and a check shirt.

'You are English, *Señorita?*'

'Well, yes . . . '

'Dance with me.' He smiled, showing beautiful white teeth. 'Please.'

And before Georgia could smilingly back off she was out in the centre of the dance-floor, being whirled round in a lively samba. When it ended she joined in the applause, breathless and laughing, but as she took a step away the young man put an arm round her.

'Please, Georgia — ' at some time in the uninhibited dance they had become

Georgia and Miguel ' — another dance.'

By some instinct, her eyes sought and found Ramón. Their glances did not meet and he was apparently deep in conversation still, although he himself did not appear to be saying very much, and she had the distinct feeling that his eyes had been withdrawn from her a split-second before hers found him. Even from this distance, though, she could see the faint frown of displeasure settling on his brows.

She hesitated, then thought, What the hell? gave him a defiant scowl and turned her back.

The next dance was a good old-fashioned rock and roll number and Georgia, who had not been quite sure of her footwork in the samba, relaxed. One of Grant's many ex-girlfriends, a lissom, leggy blonde named Samantha, had landed a job in the chorus of a rock musical a few months earlier, and had often practised at their flat, dragging Georgia through the routines with her.

And Miguel too might have come straight off the chorus line. Together, in the centre of the floor, they swayed and gyrated, and Georgia, grateful for the chance to lose herself to everything beyond the wild rhythm, the excitement racing in her blood, completely let go. Miguel, lightly gripping her waist, spun her round and round, her skirt flying, slid her between his legs and back again, then finally, as the music reached a deafening crescendo, caught her between his hands, twirled her again then held her in front of him, hard against his lean body.

After the noise there was a deafening silence for a second, then tumultuous applause and wolf-whistles, and she became aware of three things simultaneously: that they had been giving a solo performance, everyone else having drawn back, that her skirt was clinging around the tops of her bare legs, and that Ramón, his face a thundercloud, was getting to his feet, the only person in the square not applauding.

Georgia, whose breathing was just beginning to subside to normal, felt her heart lurch violently with terror as he advanced purposefully on them. He obviously thought she'd been making an exhibition of herself. He would annihilate her with his caustic tongue — and then probably Miguel with his fists.

With a last quick smile she ducked away from the young man's restraining arm, seeking the relative seclusion of their table away from the spotlit dance-floor. Ramón reached her just as she pulled out her chair and he clamped a hand over her wrist.

'We're leaving.'

In spite of her terror, the curt tone set her hackles bristling. 'Suppose I'm not ready?' she retorted, and made a grab at the chair-back.

He shook her hand free. 'Suppose you decide what's good for you.' And he began towing her between the tables and out of the square, away from the friendly warmth of other people, to plunge into the dark alley.

She tried to jerk her hand free. 'No, I won't go with you, you — you overbearing, bullying — '

'*Calla!*' he ground out between his teeth, and there was such cold venom in the snarl that she subsided into silence.

He opened the car door and reached in for his cashmere cardigan.

'Put this on. It will be cold driving through the mountains.'

'I don't want it,' she muttered sullenly. 'I'm sweltering.'

'I'm not surprised,' he replied grimly and, draping it round her shoulders, pushed her into her seat, threw himself into his own, switched on the engine with a snap which must have all but broken the key and roared off down the narrow, winding road at a speed which had her hands clenching and unclenching convulsively in her lap.

By the time he drew up at the villa, the Ferrari's nose an inch from the garage doors, she was mind-blown with the terror of that ride. But now that they were safely back her resentment began to simmer nicely again.

Climbing out, she shrugged off the cardigan and tossed it at him. 'Thanks.'

'*De nada.*'

She had intended making a silent, haughty exit, but the clipped words were like a flame to touch-paper.

'What a killjoy you are.' She faced him across the roof of the car, her chest heaving. 'Someone having a bit of harmless fun — you can't take it, can you? No one gets to have *fun* round you. No wonder Isabel packed her bags and got the hell out of it. You — '

'Be quiet.' He gestured towards the house, wrapped in darkness apart from the soft light which showed through the wrought-iron grill at the front door. 'You will wake the staff.'

'I don't care if I wake the whole damn town,' she yelled. 'You — you think I'm a wild little guttersnipe, so OK, I'll behave like one.'

'I told you, shut up,' he grated.

'Wake the staff? That's all you care about — appearances. You're so buttoned-up — No,' she cried as she saw him fling down the cardigan, 'don't you dare touch me!'

She half turned, but too late. Ramón, his face — every line in it — tight with fury, was round the car in two strides. He reached her, caught hold of her and swung her round to him.

'You little — ' He snapped off the word between his teeth, so that she never knew what it would have been.

But then, as all the tension which had been spiralling between them the whole evening finally exploded, he dragged her into his arms and kissed her, taking her mouth with savage force.

At the first impact of his lips, hot against hers, Georgia's anger vanished. Lost in the storm of assault, she clung to him, her arms around him to strain him even closer to her. They finally broke apart and stared dumbly at one another, only to kiss again as their fingers clutched, held, slid.

When he buried his mouth in the soft hollow at the base of her throat, she arched her neck for him. As his fingers closed over one breast, she gripped his back then, hungry to feel his skin against hers, pulled his shirt clear of his waistband and slipped her hands inside, closing her eyes in ecstasy as she ran her palms across his smooth back and felt the shoulder muscles tense under her.

Snatching her up, he carried her to the terrace and set her down where the padded cushions from the patio furniture had been piled. He held her away from him, though she could still feel the faint tremors running through his body. He was only controlling himself with a superhuman effort, and the knowledge intensified her own desire.

'Georgia.' He gave her a strained little smile.

'Yes?' she whispered.

'Please — undress yourself. I shall tear your clothes if I put a finger on them.'

Obediently, her eyes fixed on him, she unknotted the jersey top, her own steady fingers fumbling with it, then, as she slid out of it, heard his breath catch in his throat as he saw for the first time the tiny cream silk and lace bra which cupped her small, firm breasts.

She unhooked the catch of her skirt, slid it down and stepped out of it, seeing as she did so Ramón's eyes turn a strange, intense smoky-grey when he caught sight of the small silk briefs. Her skirt around her feet, she stood, one hand to her throat, shy, yet glorying in his expression as he took in her slim curves.

'Oh, *querida*,' he said huskily. 'My beautiful, wild, passionate girl.'

And then, almost of their own volition, it seemed, the rest of their clothes were off and they were on the soft, yielding cushions, so that for the first time in her life Georgia knew what it was to lie naked in the arms of a naked man. For the first time . . .

She had to tell him. She didn't know

how he would react when he found out. Maybe he would thrust her away even now when he discovered that she didn't after all know how to play the sophisticated love-games he thought she knew so well. She had to tell him!

'Ramón,' she whispered against his shoulder.

'Shh, my sweet.'

'But there's something I must — '

'Hush.' His warm mouth silenced her. 'Between us, the time for talking is long past.'

And as he moved over her all her misgivings melted in the heat of her love and desire for him. Having fought him for so long, in the age-old gesture of submission to the conqueror, she opened her thighs to him.

She felt him tense, then thrust, and as he pierced her there was pain, a searing knife-thrust which came so swiftly that the cry was wrenched from her throat before she could set her teeth on it. She buried her face in his shoulder to smother it, but too late.

Ramón's whole body went rigid. He lay for a moment longer, his head against her cheek, and then eased himself on to one elbow, looking down at her. When she twisted her head away, unable to meet his eyes, he gently turned her face back to his.

'Georgia?' His voice was questioning.

'What?' she muttered, her teeth still clenched on the pain.

'Why didn't you tell me?' he asked softly.

'I'm s-sorry. I know — I know I'm a total failure.' She tried to smile, caught between tears and tremulous, near-hysterical laughter.

'Oh, my — '

'I've ruined it, and I wanted it to be so wonderful for you.' If you only knew how wonderful, my darling, she added silently. 'You must think I'm some kind of a dinosaur.' She struggled to regain just a fraction of her old spirit. 'I mean — a virgin at my age. How ridiculous can you get?'

But she had to press a hand to her

mouth to stifle a sob, and Ramón, muttering something which sounded like a terrible oath, sat up, pulling her into his arms to cradle her against him, one hand stroking her curls.

'Don't, *mia amada*,' he said unsteadily. 'Was that what you were trying to tell me?'

'Mmm.' A tear rolled off her cheek and caught in one of the little hairs of his chest.

'And I wouldn't listen.' His voice was rough with suppressed emotion. 'So that, instead of cherishing you and the gift you were offering me as something infinitely precious, I violated you, hurting you just as if I had been intent on rape. Yes!' he exclaimed fiercely as she tried to stem the flow of self-recrimination.

She shivered convulsively, the sweat cooling on her clammy skin, and he got to his feet, catching her up in his arms once more. His face set, he strode indoors, up the stairs to his bedroom and through to the bathroom, where he gently set her down.

'You're cold. Would you like a bath?'

'Perhaps a shower.'

He set the water running in the tiled compartment then, his face still grim, turned as if to go. Georgia put a hand on his arm.

'Please, Ramón, stay with me.'

He was going to refuse — she saw it in his eyes. Then, as she took his hand, he followed her into the shower and, putting his arms around her, let the warm water cascade over their chilled bodies. Taking a sponge, he began stroking it very tenderly all over her shoulders, breasts, stomach, then, kneeling in front of her, the water plastering the dark hair to his skull, her legs and finally between her thighs, until his gentle touch eased away the very last of the throbbing soreness where he had torn the fragile skin.

Wrapping her in a big white bath-towel, he patted her dry as though she were a child, while she stood still, watching the rivulets of water trickling down his chest, across his belly and thighs. But all at once watching was not enough. She wanted to let her hands follow the same path, wanted to feel his taut body quicken into life for her again.

He tossed away the towel, wrapped her in another dry one, then stood gazing down at her, a strange, unreadable expression in his eyes.

'I'll take you to your bedroom. Perhaps you'd like a hot drink?'

Looking up at him, she very deliberately laid her hand on his chest; she felt his heartbeat skitter, then right itself.

'No, thank you, Ramón — and I'm staying here with you.'

His mouth twisted. 'Do you think that is wise, Georgia? On the beach the other night I deliberately set out to reject you in the cruellest way I knew. And then tonight I invaded your body brutally, as one of my ancestors would have done, no doubt.' Another bitter twist of his mouth. 'Not a very impressive track record, would you say?'

'And, of course, you knocked me out the first time we met — *and* left me for the rats in that horrible dungeon, don't forget.'

She gave him a shy, sidelong smile, then, taking his hand, raised it to her lips, turned it and kissed the palm. As it trembled slightly against her mouth, she said softly, 'Don't send me away, Ramón, not tonight. I want you to l-love me — ' her voice stumbled on the word ' — and I want to love you.'

'Oh, my sweet.'

Snatching her up, he carried her back through to his bedroom, where there was a large bed draped with a dark fur spread. Laying her down on its softness, he loosened the towel and came down beside her, then, propping himself on one elbow, gazed down at her, his eyes tender yet at the same time smoky with desire as they roved across her body.

'Ramón,' she murmured.

'Mmm?'

'It's just — well, I'm sure you're so experienced . . . '

A wry smile. 'Just a little more than you, perhaps, *querida*.'

'And now you know how inexperienced I am. So can you teach me tonight — to love, I mean?'

'To love?' He grimaced. 'I think that it is you who could give me a lesson in loving, little one. But as for the *art* of love — ' he shot her a slanted smile ' — I will teach you, with the greatest of pleasure. You begin very simply — like this . . . '

Bending over her, he began to brush his lips across hers until she closed her eyes, tiny *frissons* of desire rippling through her to every nerve-end.

'And then this . . . ' he said against her mouth as first his hands and then his lips moved to caress, stroke, linger over, circle her entire body in a sweet, seductive wooing, until at last blind passion took her over and she lay taut and trembling in his arms, frantic for release yet terrified that that release would destroy the Georgia she had been for twenty-five years.

Time and again he brought her to the very edge of that destruction then drew her back, calming her as she clung helplessly to him, before bringing her to that perilous brink again. Finally, though, he lifted his head, taking in her flushed skin, the beads of sweat on her brow, then eased himself across her, and she opened her arms eagerly to him, her body reaching up to meet his.

This time there was no pain in his possession of her, only a marvellous, slow friction of flesh against flesh as her softness yielded to his hardness — yielded, then embraced and possessed him in her turn. Ramón, his entire frame shaking slightly as he fought for control over himself, moved slowly, as though to resist the arching of her hips against his.

But then, among the barely coherent tangle of words, he caught, 'Please, Ramón — I can't bear it.'

He groaned softly in his throat, she

felt him tense, then he unleashed the power within himself, thrusting deep into her, each thrust pushing her further and further towards that ultimate brink of extinction which she craved, yet feared.

There was brilliant colour all around her, filling her, burning her brain; there was pleasure so intense that she could hardly bear it, sensation so violent that her whole being shuddered. Then, just at the last, the lights exploded in her head and she was tumbling down, over the edge of that precipice into a bottomless pit of darkness . . .

When she roused herself from oblivion, she was still alive — that fact in itself seemed incredible to her dazed mind — and lying entwined with Ramón, a film of sweat on them both. As her lashes fluttered up, it was to see that he was watching her, and she blushed.

'Well.' He gave her a smile which did not quite manage to be ironic. 'That was quite a first lesson, my sweet. No, don't.' As Georgia, the blush intensifying, tried to turn her head away, he trapped her face, tilting it to him. 'Don't be embarrassed, my sweet.'

'I'm not,' she began huskily. 'It's just that it was so much more — ' She broke off, gazing up at him, her amber eyes still brimming with the dazed wonderment she felt. 'So overwhelming.'

He returned her gaze without the hint of a smile. 'Yes, it was, wasn't it? And now, your lesson in loving so aptly learned, you lie in my arms — ' his eyes wandered lazily over her ' — eternal woman — mysterious, warm, inviting — everything a man could ever want. Soft flesh — ' one hand brushed her breasts and she bit her lip as the peaks, already bruised from his teeth and lips, tingled slightly ' — skin like cream, laced with those palest of blue veins. Such a slender, fragile, *beautiful* body, which is, I think, ready now — '

'Ready?' she prompted breathlessly as he broke off with a little cat-like smile.

'For its second, *advanced* lesson

— something along the lines of this . . . and this . . . and this . . . '

And again he worked his magical arts on her until the fires — which she knew only he could rouse — blazed up in her once more, white-hot and incandescent . . .

* * *

Ramón was asleep when she woke to see the first faint threads of daylight. She was still lying curled against him, exactly as he had gathered her to him just seconds before they had both plunged into sleep. One arm was heavy across her, but when she moved her head very cautiously she could see his face, half buried in the pillow.

The lines had gone, all smoothed out by a night of passionate lovemaking. Even that sardonic twist at one corner of his mouth, which so easily deepened into cruelty, was gone. His jaw was fuzzed with heavy black stubble, which strangely gave him an altogether softer look — made him look younger, more endearing, more human, so that she yearned to reach out and stroke it.

They were both reflected in his dressing-table mirror, her pale limbs entwined with his tanned ones. She'd imagined that she would seem changed in some subtle way this morning, but no. Her body looked no different — her hips were no less slender, her breasts no more rounded — and yet it had aroused in Ramón a passion she had never dreamed possible. That morning in his bedroom in the castle — that was when he'd first called her beautiful and had promised that he would teach her to glory in her body. Well, he had more than fulfilled that promise now . . . though there had been no pretence, of course, no empty avowals of undying love . . .

A sudden stabbing spear-thrust went through her. She loved Ramón; last night she'd given herself to him — and what now? Two weeks at the most, and Grant would be here . . .

Could she in that time make Ramón love her? No. She wasn't even sure if he was capable of really loving any woman since losing Isabel's mother, but if he ever did learn to love again one day it would be a docile, submissive woman who gained his heart, not one of the Georgia Leighs of this world, who fought him at every turn.

She ought to stop the affair now — for her own sake — but even the pain that would have helped her to be strong had faded. That would come again later, when Ramón had let her go. Now, as she looked at him, all she could feel was desire uncoiling itself inside her, the aching love which made her want to cry and in the same moment shout for happiness. Two weeks . . .

She would take the gifts they brought, with joy and gratitude — and then face whatever the future held.

All at once restless, she slid out from under Ramón's arm. He moved, murmured something, then flung himself over on to his other side, so that she was able to slip out of bed and cross to the window.

Pushing back the heavy curtains a little, she looked out. It was a glorious morning, the garden beneath the window fresh still, the flowers and shrubs not yet hanging their heads in the searing heat. Nothing moved except a flock of white gulls swooping over the beach and, far away on the main road, one little car, a small red Seat.

She watched it idly, but then with more interest as it turned off the road down the narrow track leading to La Herradura, then swung into the private drive which led to the villa. It came cautiously, as if the driver was not quite sure where he or she was heading, rounded the last clump of cypresses and pulled up just below the window from which she was watching.

The driver's door opened, and Georgia, her eyes dilating with astonishment, gave a strangled gasp. Then, snatching up the nearest garment — Ramón's robe — she hurtled downstairs, scrambling herself into it. She reached the front door just as the first harsh ring of the bell pealed through the house, unbolted it and flung it open.

'Grant! What on earth are you doing here?'

10

'I might ask the same of you,' her brother retorted, then, as Georgia appeared incapable of movement, he pushed back the front door, walked into the hall and swung round to face her. 'What's going on, Georgy?'

And quite suddenly she woke up to the fact that her twin — her beloved other half — was in deadly danger, was standing in Ramón Torres's hall, and Ramón Torres had made terrible threats against him.

'No,' she babbled in an urgent whisper, clutching hold of his arm, 'you mustn't stay, Grant. It — it isn't safe. You must go — *now.*'

'Isn't *safe*?' he repeated, a slight frown settling between his brows. 'Georgy, are you all right — you haven't got a touch of the sun or anything?'

'No, of course not.' She pushed the

question aside impatiently. 'But how did you know I was here? I thought you were sailing round the Med still.' Hardly realising it, she was whispering again.

Grant pulled a wry face. 'I should have been — if it weren't for the guy who'd chartered the yacht. As soon as his back was turned, some smart operator took the chance to launch a take-over bid for his company. Boy, no one, but no one, has ever got back to Marbella in such double-quick time.'

As he gave a reminiscent laugh, she clutched his arm convulsively again. 'Shh!'

The frown deepened, but he went on more quietly, 'Last night I was in Mike's bar — you remember, down by the waterfront? — and I met up with two girls I know. They asked me if I'd got a twin sister, because they'd seen this girl — my look-alike — eating in a restaurant in Nerja with a man one of them recognised as Ramón Torres.'

Of course, Georgia thought, those

two chic young women — she'd thought they'd been eyeing her out of sheer astonishment that a man like Ramón could lower himself to be seen with her . . .

'Apparently the father of one of them crossed this Torres character in business a few years ago and still regrets it. This is his villa, isn't it?' He fixed his sister with a stern eye.

'Well — yes.'

She felt the warm colour flood into her cheeks as he appeared to register for the first time the oversized robe which was falling off her bare shoulders.

'And is he here?'

'Yes — er — yes, he is. But look, Grant, he thinks you — '

'What the hell is going on here?'

A chill voice came from the bend of the staircase, and two heads of copper curls swivelled automatically, to see Ramón coming down it, barefoot, tucking a white shirt into his jeans. At the bottom of the stairs he halted abruptly, looking from one to the other, then whistled softly through his teeth.

'*Dios*! The resemblance is — remarkable.'

Two pairs of identical amber eyes stared at him, then two identical halves of one whole separated. One half put a hand involuntarily to its throat, while the other scowled belligerently at him.

'Yes, what the hell is going on, Torres — I take it you are Ramón Torres?'

Georgia sucked in her breath. Surely no one had ever dared to speak to Ramón in that insolent tone and lived to tell the tale?

'Grant!' Blind terror was gripping her lungs, making it all but impossible for her to speak. 'Grant, he thinks you made his niece — '

'That is enough, Georgia.' Ramón's icy voice silenced her. 'This matter is entirely between your brother and myself. Go to your room.'

Go to her room? Sent away like a naughty schoolgirl? After what they'd shared — the passion, the savage joy of possessing one another? An hysterical laugh bubbled up in her, but then, as Ramón advanced on them both, she flung herself in front of her twin, eyes flashing fire, all her old fierce protectiveness instantly welling up.

'Don't touch him, Ramón. If you hurt him, I'll — I'll — '

'Shut up, Georgy,' her brother snapped. As he pushed her out of the way, his eyes took in the man-sized robe again, and he turned to glare at Ramón. 'I don't know what's been going on here, Torres — '

'I promise you, Grant — ' Georgia was looking directly at Ramón, holding his gaze unwaveringly ' — that nothing has happened here that I did not want to happen.'

'Oh, so it's like that, is it?' Grant's mouth twisted slightly and his gaze ranged between them both. 'Well, I suppose you're a big girl now, Georgy. But,' he went on, homing in on Ramón again, 'I promise you, Torres, if you've harmed a hair on my sister's head, I'll — '

'Oh, not you too.' Ramón held up a hand. 'Please, this is becoming boring.'

Jamming his thumbs into the belt of his jeans, he surveyed Grant's angry face, and his build, so much slighter than his own. Even so, Georgia saw her twin's fists bunch at his sides, and put in hurriedly, 'Grant — he thinks you took his niece away — '

'Seduced her away,' a cold voice interposed.

' — with you after you stopped off in his village last time.'

'His niece? What the hell are you talking about?'

'Isabel Torres — that is who I'm talking about.' Ramón's voice was, if possible, even more arctic. 'She was seen riding out of the village on the back of your motorbike, so do not try to deny it.'

'Oh.' The puzzled frown cleared and Grant chuckled. 'Isabel — quite a girl, that one. Yes, I gave her a lift — she begged me for one, in fact. Was desperate to get away from her guardian who, I gather, is a real old-fashioned chauvinist, Spanish variety . . . ' He caught sight of his sister's face and the sentence tailed away abruptly. 'That's you, I suppose.'

'I am her guardian, yes,' Ramón agreed levelly. 'So — where is she now?' the silky voice probed.

'I've no idea. Sorry.'

'Don't lie to me.' There was no silk in the voice now. 'She is with you in Marbella.'

'With me?' Grant laughed incredulously. 'Good grief, of course she isn't. I haven't set eyes on her since I dropped her off twenty miles down the road — ' He broke off. 'My bike — where is it?'

Ramón waved a hand irritably. 'At my other house. But this story — you really expect me to believe it?'

Grant shrugged. 'Suit yourself — it's the truth. Wild sixteen-year-olds don't hold much attraction for me these days — Georgia's teenage years were more than enough for me.'

He grinned easily, but Ramón remained stony-faced.

'Hang on a minute, though,' Grant went on. 'I think I do know where she is.'

He disappeared, and they heard his light footsteps running down the steps, then the car door opening. Georgia's glance met Ramón's, his face unreadable, then, as Grant came back up the steps, her eyes slid away.

'Thought I had this in my jacket pocket.' He thrust a crumpled postcard at Ramón. 'My Spanish isn't great, but — well, read it.' To Georgia he added, 'She's in Madrid.'

His sister nodded, but her gaze never left Ramón, who skimmed through the card then handed it back to Grant.

'I remember now,' Grant went on, 'when I dropped her off that day a boy — a student she'd met while he was fruit-picking in the village — was waiting for her. They were going to Madrid together. She . . . ' he hesitated

' . . . she said her guardian would never have allowed her to go there to study, so that was the only way. She intends to get her exams and train as a vet — she adores animals, apparently.'

They were both watching Ramón and saw him nod slowly. 'Yes, she loves all animals — especially horses — just as Luisa, her mother, did.'

At the pain in his voice, Georgia's tender heart ached to go over to him, put her arms round him, hold him to her and comfort him. But that was impossible now . . . He turned to her.

'It seems, Georgia, that I owe you an apology,' he said formally. 'You were right — and I was wrong.'

'So you believe Grant?' Her spirits lifted with relief.

'Yes.' There was a long pause. 'If only because it is exactly what Luisa would have done. Señor Leigh — ' he turned back to Grant ' — you will stay — have breakfast — and then I will tell you precisely where your motorcycle is.'

'I'd rather get on, thanks. Adela did

me sandwiches, which I had back along the road.'

'Adela?' Georgia queried.

'Yes, my — er — fiancée.' Her twin almost blushed. 'We met on the charter — she was the cook. That's the other reason I came looking for you. We're getting married next week in Marbella, and you must be bridesmaid.'

'Married? Oh, Grant.' She smiled at him, a smile which blurred suddenly as a tiny stab of pain, jealousy even, went through her. Never again would she come first with her adored brother. But then she put her arms around him and hugged him. 'I'm so glad — and yes, of course, I'd love to be Adela's bridesmaid.' She kissed his cheek, then aimed a playful punch at his stomach. 'It's high time you settled down.'

'Yeah, that's what Adela says.' He grinned, rumpling his curls boyishly. 'I can't wait for you to meet her — I know you'll love her.'

Georgia gave Ramón a swift glance. He was standing, quite impassive, his eyes on them both, and at the implacability in his face her heart fell like lead into a bottomless pit. It was over — all over — and so . . .

'Grant,' she said unsteadily. 'I'll come with you now. I've been working for Señor Torres — some landscaping designs — but they're more or less finished, so there's n-nothing to keep me here now.'

Her brother's gaze flickered to Ramón for a moment then back to her. 'Are you quite sure of that, Georgy?'

'Quite sure.' But her voice threatened to break again and she hurried on, 'And anyway, I'm dying to meet Adela. Give me ten minutes.'

'Just time for me to offer your brother a coffee, then,' Ramón put in smoothly as she walked past him to the staircase, but she could not look at him.

In her bedroom she leaned up against the door as her stiff face began to crumple. I will not cry, she told herself fiercely, and blindly started cramming her things into her bag — her own things, nothing that he had bought her. When she came to take off his robe, though, she cradled it in her arms for a few moments. It felt soft and warm, and smelled faintly of him. Then, as her mouth began to tremble again, she laid it carefully down on the bed and went through for a shower . . .

There was no one in the hall when she came back downstairs. She stood listening, but no sounds came from the dining-room, and when she opened the glass doors the terrace was deserted. This was where, last night . . . No, she must shut her mind to all that. Ramón wasn't even going to bother to say goodbye to her.

A flight of steps led from the terrace to the drive. She went halfway down, then stopped dead. There was no sign of Grant, and the red Seat had gone; only Ramón was standing there, arms propped on the ornamental railings, staring down at the Mediterranean.

As she halted, he turned and watched her come down the rest of the steps.

'Where's Grant?' she demanded, then, as suspicion flared in her, 'You did believe him, didn't you? You haven't —?'

'Don't worry. He is on his way to the castle to collect his beloved Rudge-Whitworth.'

'You've sent him away!' Her voice rose in accusation. 'He'd never have gone without me. Now look here — ' dropping her bag on the tiles, she glared up at him, her eyes flashing amber sparks ' — you can't hold me prisoner any longer.'

He shook his head slightly. 'You are staying, Georgia.'

'No.' She couldn't stay. It was like tearing herself in half to leave him now. If she couldn't escape now, she would bleed to death inside when she finally had to wrench herself away. 'No — that wasn't part of the bargain. You said you'd keep me until Grant came — '

'Ah, but I am afraid the rules of the game have changed slightly. And in any case, we still have some unfinished business, you and I.'

'But you heard what I said to Grant. The plans are more or less complete — anyone could take them over now.'

'You are coming with me to Madrid.'

'Don't you ever listen?' She banged her hands down on the railings, wincing as their sharp edge hurt her palms. 'I don't need to see those architects again, so — '

'No, not them. We are both going to see Isabel.'

She stared at him, momentarily taken aback. 'Oh, but — '

'She was, after all, the cause of our first — encounter.' He gave her a rather wry smile that she could not respond to. 'It appears from her card that she is living with that young man's parents, but it would be more fitting for her to move to a young women's hostel.'

'So,' Georgia said slowly, 'you aren't going to make her come back with you?'

'No, she will study as she wishes, and become a vet. I see now that I was somewhat — over-protective towards her, perhaps because she is so much like her mother, and no one could ever curb her wild spirit.'

'And is that why . . . ?' Her voice tailed off.

'Why I set out to tame you? Perhaps — but also, no doubt — ' there was a glint in those pale grey eyes ' — because I am an arrogant, overbearing chauvinist — Spanish variety.'

'Well, maybe.' Georgia had the grace to blush slightly, but then went on earnestly, 'You do see, though, that people have to be free to make their own mistakes.'

'Yes — although there is one mistake I do not intend making.' His voice was silky. 'You told me once that I behave exactly as I choose — well, I choose to keep you.'

Just how cruel could he be? He must know how she felt about him. 'For h-how much longer?'

'Well, shall we say — in the first

instance — fifty years?'

'Fifty . . . ?' Georgia's eyes almost swallowed the rest of her face. She gulped, then went on in a low, unsteady voice, 'Don't tease me, Ramón. I — I can't bear it.'

'I'm not teasing you, little one.' Suddenly that hateful silky note was gone, to be replaced by a tenderness which made her stomach constrict. 'I want you to marry me.'

'You mean — ' she could barely get the words out ' — you want me to be your wife?'

He shot her a ragged little smile. 'Well, that is what marrying usually means.' He paused, then continued, a wholly new note of uncertainty in his voice. 'You do love me, don't you, Georgia? Surely the message I've been receiving from those beautiful, expressive eyes cannot be wrong?'

'Yes, Ramón.' Georgia looked up at him, all her love at last shimmering unfettered in her gaze. 'Of course I do. But — ' her eyes clouded suddenly

' — you don't love me. You think I'm wild — you need a docile, obedient wife. You — ' She stopped as, like lightning, a terrible suspicion flared in her, then she went on stiffly, 'You don't have to marry me just because you . . . '

'Brutally deflowered you?' he completed as she hesitated. 'No, I know I don't. I want to marry you, *mia amada*, because I love you.'

'You — love — me?' Georgia stared blankly at him, and saw for the first time, behind the arrogance and the self-assurance of a man who must always demand his own way, a vulnerability which twisted at her insides. 'Really love me?' she added rather wistfully.

'Really love you, forever.' He gave her a faint, strained smile, then, as her face began to pucker, pulled her into his arms, holding her tightly to him. 'You affect me like no other woman I have ever met,' he murmured huskily against her curls. 'I can't bear you out of my sight. I want to be with you always. I want to see you when I wake, and be with you when I sleep. I want to take care of you, see you grow big with my child, cherish you forever. You are in my blood — ' he twined his finger in one of her curls and tugged it gently ' — and I shall never get you out until I die. So — what do you say?'

Easing her away a fraction, he looked down at her, and Georgia, her eyes like stars, met his gaze, half loving, half full of that sombre uncertainty.

'I say yes, please, Ramón.'

'Oh, my darling.'

And as her fingers fluttered up to his face he seized her hand and buried his face in the palm, smothering it with kisses of pure love.

11

As Ramón brought the big Range Rover to a halt, Georgia climbed out and went across to the rail, eager for that first glimpse of the much loved view. Below her the Mediterranean sparkled in the late afternoon sun which cast long, inviting shadows across the landscaped gardens. Her husband came up beside her and slipped his arm around her shoulders.

'Well, *querida*, and are you finally satisfied with it?'

'I think so. Although I still wonder if I should have that bridge moved a — '

'Oh, no,' Ramón groaned. 'What did I ever do to deserve such a perfectionist? Please — not that bridge again. I have been telling you for four years now, it is just right.'

As he rumpled her hair — worn slightly longer now, the curls framing her delicate features — she laughed up at him. 'All right, I agree — it's fine where it is. I can't quite see the cascade, though, now that the bamboo's grown up.'

She stood on tiptoe and Ramón released her. 'Go on down and have a closer look.'

'Oh, no, I'll wait for you.'

'Yes, you go on to the pool — I'll join you there.' He gave her a little push. 'I have a couple of phone calls to make, and it will do you good to get some peace and quiet for a while. Heaven knows — ' he glanced at the back seat of the Range Rover, then rolled his eyes expressively ' — you get little enough of either these days.'

Georgia followed one of the tiled pathways which meandered down through La Herradura, turning aside to see the little central plaza. Bougainvillaea, scarlet and peach, foamed over the white walls, and through the ornamental wrought-iron gates she could glimpse pretty gardens, with guests sitting on their shady patios. A group of small children — a polyglot of nationalities, to judge from the babble — were playing around the fountain and paddling in the stream which flowed out of it and went tumbling down the hillside.

She turned down another path and the plaza was hidden behind a trellis of blue morning-glory, the children's shrill voices fading. Down by the pool it was cool in the shade of the eucalyptus, whose graceful branches filtered the sunlight, and she stood for a few minutes, feeling the beauty and peace of the place settle on her.

She had created other gardens, of course, before and since. The one for that Brennan hotel was considered by many to be her masterpiece, and took pride of place in her portfolio — though privately she preferred the garden she'd laid out last year for Grant and Adela at their new villa near Marbella. But this garden was special to her. So much love had gone into its creation that her feelings for it ran very deep, so deep that only Ramón guessed at them.

Past the pool was an archway, beyond that another splashy little waterfall with some stepping-stones across the stream, and alongside it, set against a mossy bank, was a rustic seat. She went up to it, meaning to sit down there and wait for Ramón, but then stopped dead. In the rock, just beside where the water came trickling over the lip, was an oval marble plaque, and carved into it were the words '*ARQUITECTA* — GEORGIA TORRES'.

'You've found it, then?' As Ramón put his arms round her from behind, she turned to him.

'It's a wonderful surprise.' She gave him a blurred smile, then, pulling his face down to hers, kissed him. 'Is this my fourth wedding anniversary present you promised me? Thank you, darling.'

'Part of it. Here's the rest.' Releasing her, he dug a slim white leather box out of his hip-pocket. 'I thought it would match your eyes rather well,' he added casually.

When she opened the box, into her hands spilled a long necklace of polished amber, the pieces set in a heavy, intricately worked chain of dark gold.

'Oh, Ramón, it's lovely.' She bit her lip. 'But you give me so much.'

'Not half as much as you give me.' With his little finger he gently brushed across her wide mouth, her lips parted in a tremulous smile, then, taking the necklace, he hooked it round her neck so that it fell between her breasts. 'Of course a white blouse is fine, but for best effect it should be seen against that creamy skin of yours.' Their eyes met, a long, lingering look redolent of all their shared pleasures. 'Oh, *mia amada* . . . ' he began huskily, his hands tightening on her shoulders.

'No — I want to.'

From the path just behind them there was a yelp, a scuffle, then, as they both swung round, a loud, indignant wail. Two children — a boy of three years old and a little girl a year or so younger, in smart navy and white sailor suits and white soft leather boots — had sat down with a crash on the bank. The toddler had obviously launched herself at the boy, for she was sprawling all over him.

'*Niños!*' As two small heads swivelled, Ramón strode over to them.

'Papá.' The little girl, tears spilling from huge amber eyes, was gazing piteously up at her father. 'F'lipe pushed me.'

'I don't think so, *mia pequeña*.'

'Sí. He did — he did.'

Scowling at her brother, she grabbed a fat handful of copper curls and tugged hard, until finally her brother thumped her with a small though determined fist.

'*Calla!*' Going down on his haunches, Ramón shook an admonishing finger at his indignant daughter.

'He did push me.' Another angry tear welled over.

'Now, *querida*.' As Georgia watched,

287

struggling not to laugh, he went on severely, 'You know, I think if there was any pushing you were doing more than your share. Poor Felipe — '

'But I wanted to go first.' A tiny jaw jutted pugnaciously. 'He always goes first.'

'Across there?' Ramón glanced doubtfully at the line of slippery, moss-covered stepping-stones. 'But you cannot go across them.'

'*Sí*, Papá, I can. Look at me.'

As the toddler wiped her grubby hands down her immaculate sailor suit and stepped precariously out on to the first stone, he made an instinctive move to snatch her from it. But then, meeting his wife's eye, he gave her a wry little smile and held back, staying just close enough to catch the child if she fell.

'I did it! I crossed it all on my own, Elena.'

The little girl laughed up in triumph at a young, sweet-faced Spanish girl who was coming down the path, carrying two tiny matching red buckets and spades. Ramón, laughing too, caught up both children and hugged them to him.

'Kiss for Papá.' Two chubby pairs of lips pouted in a soft kiss. 'And for Mamá.' Georgia put up her face for two more feather-soft kisses, then he set them down.

'Now go with Elena to make sandcastles. We shall be down to inspect them in ten minutes.'

They stood watching as, one hand of each clinging to Elena, the other clutching bucket and spade, the children went off. At the corner they turned, gave their parents identical cherubic smiles, then disappeared.

Ramón expelled a long breath. '*Dios*, what a pair — and what did we do before Elena arrived to help out? But little Ana, will she ever improve, do you think?'

They exchanged rueful glances, then Georgia laughed. 'Well, I did, didn't I?'

'Yes,' her husband agreed thoughtfully, 'but not until you were at least twenty-five. I seem to remember telling you then that the world had room for only one Georgia Leigh — but I did not reckon with a second copper-curled little moppet.' He smiled at her tenderly. 'And you like your anniversary gift?'

'Oh, yes.' She looked down at the necklace, then sighed.

'That was a deep sigh, my sweet.'

'Oh, I was just thinking how lucky I am. A wonderful husband, adorable children.'

He took her hand. 'It's I who am lucky, my love. I have you, and Ana and Felipe.'

Just for a moment, the fierce, possessive love blazed up in his eyes, and Georgia studied him, taking in every detail of his beloved face.

'Ramón,' she began huskily, 'I have a present for you too.'

'But all I want is you.'

'You know I've been feeling a bit tired —'

'I'm not surprised, with those two terrors.' He pulled a face. 'I don't feel too good myself sometimes.'

'Well, I went to see Doctor Molina

yesterday.' She paused. 'I'm pregnant, Ramón.'

'Pregnant?' he repeated softly. 'Oh, my darling.' His voice was unsteady as he took her in his arms. 'Thank you, my love. That's the most wonderful present you could have given me.'

Bending his head, he kissed her, very gently at first, all his protective tenderness keeping his passion in check. But then, as always, the fire between them ignited, and they clung to one another, only breaking apart as a couple came up the winding path from the beach.

When they had gone, Ramón grinned wryly down at her. '*Dios!*' He ran a hand through his hair. 'Married to you for four years, and I still can't keep my hands off you for more than ten minutes at a time. Do you think I shall ever improve, *querida*?'

Georgia appeared to ponder the question. 'I don't really know,' she replied demurely. 'I do hope not.' And he took her in his arms again.

We do hope that you have enjoyed reading this large print book.

Did you know that all of our titles are available for purchase?

We publish a wide range of high quality large print books including:
Romances, Mysteries, Classics
General Fiction
Non Fiction and Westerns

Special interest titles available in large print are:
The Little Oxford Dictionary
Music Book, Song Book
Hymn Book, Service Book

Also available from us courtesy of Oxford University Press:
Young Readers' Dictionary
(large print edition)
Young Readers' Thesaurus
(large print edition)

For further information or a free brochure, please contact us at:
Ulverscroft Large Print Books Ltd.,
The Green, Bradgate Road, Anstey,
Leicester, LE7 7FU, England.
Tel: (00 44) **0116 236 4325**
Fax: (00 44) **0116 234 0205**

OUT OF THE SHADOWS

Catriona McCuaig

Newly single and enjoying her job as an office temp, Rowena Dexter sees new hope for the future when she starts dating barrister Tom Forrest. But memories of a terrifying childhood incident resurface when she receives threatening e-mails. She was in the house when her aunt was murdered, and the case has never been solved. Rowena's former husband, Bruce, agrees to help her unmask the stalker, but can they solve the mystery before the murderer strikes again?

CHATEAU OF THE WINDMILL

Sheila Benton

Hannah's employer, a public relations agency, has despatched her to France to handle the promotion of a Chateau which is to be converted to an hotel. However Gerrard, the son of the owner, resents the conversion, and some of the residents of the Chateau are not what they seem to be. Now she begins to find herself entangled both in a mystery that surrounds a valuable tapestry, and also a Frenchman's romantic intentions . . .

BRAVE HEART

Diney Delancey

Glad to be leaving London and
many unhappy memories, Janine
Sherwood moves to Friars Bridge to
take up her post as headmistress of
the village school. Living in th
house owned by school governor S
Gavin Hampton, Janine and he
daughter Tamsyn are comfortabl
establis ed there. But shadows from
the p   reach out to haunt her
— threatening to shatter the happiness she and Tamsyn have found.
Danger surrounds Janine as she
fights to save all she holds most
dear.